LET THERE BE BLOOD

By Jane Jakeman

IN THE KINGDOM OF MISTS

The Lord Ambrose Mysteries

LET THERE BE BLOOD
THE EGYPTIAN COFFIN
FOOL'S GOLD

LET THERE BE
*B*LOOD

JANE JAKEMAN

BERKLEY PRIME CRIME, NEW YORK

A Berkley Prime Crime Book
Published by The Berkley Publishing Group
A division of Penguin Group (USA) Inc.
375 Hudson Street
New York, New York 10014

This book is an original publication of The Berkley Publishing Group.

LET THERE BE BLOOD

A Berkley Prime Crime book / published by arrangement with the author

PRINTING HISTORY
Headline Book Publishing paper edition / 1997
Berkley Prime Crime trade edition / 2004

Copyright © 1997 by Jane Jakeman.

Cover design by George Long.
Interior text design by Kristin del Rosario.

First American edition: September 2004
Previously published in Great Britain in 1997 by Headline Book Publishing.

Library of Congress Cataloging-in-Publication Data

Jakeman, Jane.
    Let there be blood / Jane Jakeman.—Berkley Prime Crime trade ed.
        p. cm.
    ISBN 0-425-19812-X
    1. Greece—History—War of Independence, 1821-1829—
Veterans—Fiction. 2. Aristocracy (Social class)—Fiction.
3. Farmers—Crimes against—Fiction. 4. Somerset (England)—
Fiction. 5. Recluses—Fiction. 6. Romanies—Fiction. I. Title.

PR6060.A435L47 2004
823'.92—dc22
                                                2004047622

PRINTED IN THE UNITED STATES OF AMERICA

10 9 8 7 6 5 4 3 2 1

For J. M.
and in memory of P. and C.

"Let there be light," said God, "and there was Light!"
"Let there be Blood!" says man, and there's a sea!

Byron, Don Juan, *Canto VII, Stanza XLI*

Turnpike

Westmorland
Park

Anderton
Hall

Church

To Callerton

Malfi

The Mansion of

Road

Alehouse

Crawshay's
Farm

Park

Village

Icehouse

Woods

Lake

...alfine in the County of Somerset

Map by Marion Cox.

ENGLAND, 1830

CHAPTER 1

IN the shimmering heat, I saw from my library window that there were men coming up my drive. Two men from the village stumping fearfully along, breathless, their mouths open, their red faces contorted with expressions of fear and horror. They were bewildered, that was the truth. Like silly sheep searching for a shepherd, dumb innocents looking for any kind of authority, they came to me. That was the first I knew of the killings, when those round-faced country bumpkins dragged me back to the grubby business of humanity.

I have little contact with the world and have shunned it as much as I can, ever since my return from Greece, believing that I do my neighbours and myself a favour thereby. Scarred as I am, I am not a pretty sight and the young ladies hereabouts would wince in horror if they saw my face at their rustic dances and country amusements. Belos, my manservant, drives the gentry away when they call on me, and, to tell the truth, there is nowhere to receive them. The rooms have all fallen into decay, except for the few that Belos has cleared out for our residence. He and I are the only permanent dwellers in this great place. You can follow me, as I walk through my mansion of Malfine, through room after darkened room, and judge whether it is suitable for a polite gathering of local society. The reception rooms, the ballroom, the dining rooms, the grand suites and bedrooms, the endless hutches for maids up in the attics of the house, where dust, the beggar's velvet, drifts across the floors. All is deserted; the moonlight is falling through the chinks in the shutters, touching on faded marble and gilded cornices, on inlaid chests and brass-bound cabinets, glistening on the pendant milky drops of cobweb-bound chandeliers. Brocade and velvet curtains hang at the windows, all torn and rotting. The curtains are left as they were: if they were open twenty years ago, when the house was abandoned, they cannot now be drawn, for they are so decayed they would fall apart.

And if they were left drawn across the windows they cannot be opened. The rooms behind them are in permanent darkness. The silks and ruffles of my sister's bedroom. And my mother's rooms, her scent still drifting through them on warm nights, rising from her skirts and cloaks in chests and armoires, still packed away, as they were twenty years ago.

If the gentry do not call, the rustics shun me and all my works. I know that rumours circulate in the village, for Belos occasionally calls in at the tavern and listens to the talk. He holds that it is always safer to be aware of the feelings in the neighbourhood where one lives, to keep an ear to the ground as we would say, and the feelings towards me are compounded largely, it seems, of superstition and fear. For the rustics, I am the scarred and mysterious lord of the manor, no bluff squire such as they are used to. I leave them alone, and that troubles them—I do not sit on the magistrate's bench, or chaff their clod-hopping daughters or demand they till my fields. I do not give them porter and mince pies at Christmas. I have no lady who dishes out repulsive bowls of gruel to relieve their wretched old creatures, nor do I have a good old dowager mother who amuses herself by dosing their sick and palsied with noxious remedies. The common people keep away from my doors. Belos turns the nobility from the front of my mansion, the villagers do not dare to approach the servants' entrance at the back, and so my reputation as the hermit of Malfine grows.

Yet I cannot totally escape the world. News of outside events occasionally reaches us here, although I shun society. Belos is sent from time to time on an errand to a banker or merchant, and usually returns with some tittle-tattle, sometimes with a newspaper no more than a few days old, perhaps the *Morning Chronicle* or *The Times;* the sole effect of perusing them is to confirm me in my dislike of human company.

Only a month before the murders at Crawshay's farm, I had learned of the death of that Most Sovereign Heap of fat and satin, His Gracious Majesty King George the Fourth, the old rake who had ruled first as Regent and then as King in his own right, till at last he succumbed, a mountain of flesh, in June of this year. His doctors had issued a bulletin explaining that the old despot had difficulty in breathing, and then that he could no longer hold a pen to sign a document. Finally, after they had punctured his legs like cooks putting sausages on a spit, to try to draw off the dropsy that bloated his limbs, those educated horse-butchers announced his imminent decease, and he finally bust a blood vessel in a fit of coughing.

Now we are ruled by that dreary creature, William, the fourth of that name, plain in dress and manners, and a new age of dullness descends, for, gross obscenity though George the Fourth may have been, in his youth he was an ardent and lively prince. He was a lover of art, the only monarch since King Charles the First to care tuppence for a picture, unless it showed some naked nymph or bare-bottomed cherub being rammed by a hairy satyr, and left behind him the biggest collection of works of art ever assembled in this benighted island. In his youth, there were ideas of liberty current in the land, ideas such as have never flourished before nor since in this kingdom.

As a young man, of good family and the heir to a great

inheritance, I sat at his dining table. I was even present at that famous banquet where a stream with live goldfish in it ran down the centre of the table. Talk and wine flowed freely there, and I had the dreams of youth; in those days men talked of things now long forgotten, of revolution, of freedom from tyranny. Shelley and Byron—ah! my heroes then— scribbled of the golden future that lay ahead for all mankind if we could be freed from the despotism of Church and Monarchy. That was the time when my mother's country of Greece sought its liberty from Turkish rule.

But why should all this concern me now? I am, after all, the heir to an English estate, to Malfine, with its thousand acres, its lake, its coverts and spinneys, even to the very ground on which the villagers toil, the earth on which they squat, the furrows where they till their wretched living. A man cannot shit but I own the very soil beneath him—and probably the shit as well, if my lawyers had their way. Because of this, this engagement with the world that even my hermit's existence in Malfine represents, I am thus hopelessly enmeshed in the toils of life.

And I cannot leave here. The decayed melancholy of the place suits me exactly. I cannot bear to rebuild, but I cannot let it fall apart, either, cannot let the house where I grew up, the land where I ran wild as a boy, go to absolute rack and ruin. As for signing and sealing it away, selling it to strangers, that is beyond my power, for the land is entailed.

Thus, after my return from Greece, in due course I had to receive a lawyer, with a fat white dough of a face and eyes like blackcurrants sunk into a pudding. From my library window I saw him draw up, and as he got out of his carriage, I prepared myself. The scars on my face were still raw so I took pity upon him. I wrapped a black kerchief across my jaws and waved him to a chair at my mahogany library table; he was seated directly opposite me, and I took much amusement from his fearful determination to look away from my face.

He kept his gaze fixed on the wooden panelling behind me as he told me I could not sell my inheritance, no, nor gift it away, nor deed it away: this pile of masonry, the mansion of Malfine, was slung round my neck like an albatross, a weight that I must bear for the rest of my life, such as that might be.

So be it. Malfine would shelter me, and I would bear the burden.

I signed papers, issued orders. A bailiff was hired to execute my instructions concerning the grounds. Some of the overgrown fields and thickets have been cleared, though the foxes still race through the knotted woods, their high, yapping barks resounding on summer nights, their cubs leaping and snapping as they dance for me in the moonlight round the velvet clearings and the silver pools of Malfine. A few streams run clean again, the rotting sedges have been cleared from the lake. The roof of the house may collapse next year, or the year after, but, with any luck, not this year, though water still runs down the old silk wallpaper of the ballroom in a heavy rainfall and the winter winds blow like demons through the tumbling chimneys.

And these tiny involvements, the lawyer and the bailiff and the dredging of the streams, these hair-thin cracks in my fortress against the world, these tiny gaps in my defences, caught me up in the world, in all the business of murder and justice and law which I could not escape even here at Malfine. Because they knew of my return, knew there was a master at the great house, the men from the village came to me at Malfine that day, the day of the August killings, the day of the blood and heat when the corpses were already blown and moving with the busy flies.

CHAPTER 2

❧ ❧

THE dust flew up from my horse's hooves along the track to the farm. The soil hereabouts is poor and sandy at the best of times and after a dry summer it is almost like powder. This summer had been the hottest in living memory, the green fields parched and withered—it was a summer that reminded me of Crete, of that dry and dusty land of yellow rocks and mauve-tinted mountains where I had once fought and bled. England did not seem like England at all, so parched was it, so unlike the verdant and lush country one pictures at the thought of an English landscape. In the Malfine estate, the ground opened up in great cracks where streams had run dry, and on the neighbouring pastures cattle lay in wretchedness in the fields, keeping in the shade of the trees, tormented by flies. The land was a brownish-gold and as I rode along there was a haze of heat and dust hanging over all, the soil, the scrubby hedges and the Crawshay farmhouse in the distance.

The farmhouse is at least three miles from the village: a strange old place I remembered from my childhood, a great long timbered house like a galleon, an antiquity in this year of grace eighteen hundred and thirty. The wooden beams bowed out like ships' timbers and the old casements and timbered eaves jutted out over the paths around the house like the oaken forecastle of a great vessel overhanging the waters around the ship.

I could hear, as I urged Zaraband along the track from the manor towards an outbuilding, mutters and shouts that resolved themselves into men's voices: angry, raging. And then the smell reached me on the hot air—blown with the fine sandy dust—a sweet, sickening odour. Zaraband snorted and kicked up her heels at the stench, but we pressed on towards the farm and clattered into the cobbled yard.

There was a man tied to the wheel of a cart, lashed around the massive crude wooden rim.

I had seen this before. The cruellest form of mob justice, summary retribution handed out for murder. Death by the wheel.

But I had not seen in it England. I had not thought they had fallen to this barbarity in my own country. Evidently times had changed, and new cruelties had been learnt here, things that would go unpunished in this remote countryside where law depended on the whim of the local magistrate. New cruelties had been learned in the wars England had fought recently, new tortures from the men who had fought Napoleon's troops in Portugal and seen the mutilations and carnage inflicted there, new barbarisms from men who had themselves suffered from the cat or the triangle, and been discharged upon their native countryside to live as best they could. Or as worst as they could. As I recall, not long since a soldier was sentenced by a court martial to four hundred lashes for stealing a silver spoon from the officers' mess. His backbone was laid open, and he was tied to an open cart and sent jolting home, dying slowly inch by inch on the track that led north.

I too was one of those disillusioned returners from a

different world. I too, like a discharged soldier, now roamed my lands with bitterness in my heart and the knowledge of cruelties hidden in my brain.

As I rode towards Crawshay's, such thoughts of the past were uppermost in my mind, but I knew also that for my own health I must get my musings back into the present. Those two anxious yokels who had come to Malfine had informed me of the only intriguing event that had taken place in the neighbourhood during my long convalescence: the deaths in this present life, not of a gallant band of heroes, but of two perfectly uninteresting and commonplace country farmers. Dull boors, no doubt, for whom life had been a sodden heap of toil and rough pleasures, and who would probably have died in some drunken quarrel, or fighting over a miserable bag of copper coins or an alehouse slut.

The man on the wheel had been tied with his back arched around the rim, lashed to the spokes, so that when they started to turn, the rim would crush his bones into the ground under the weight of the cart. The wheel would move an inch at a time, crushing first his feet, and then his legs, and then would turn slowly, slowly, with his face moving inexorably towards the ground. He would be conscious enough to see the earth coming up towards him as he screamed and begged for mercy and his blood spurted out into the thirsty earth of the cart-track.

He was a dark man, brown-faced, covered in sweat and dust, with a ragged shirt and breeches and a red neckerchief around the powerful throat. His face was grazed and his upper lip had been split open by a blow from a fist. Blood had trickled down upon his shirt.

"Steady—steady now, back her in, back up there!"

A small red-haired creature, wiry and busy, was directing the others. A great cart-horse was being urged between the shafts, bucking and tossing, terrified of the smell, the rage, the shouts.

I glanced round to take in the scene. The men stood about the cart in a threatening band, their faces twisted with hatred. One man alone was aloof from the mob: fair-haired and open-faced, he stood at a distance, his arms folded, his face impassive. Like the rest, he wore a rough countryman's shirt and britches, but his bearing was different: he held himself upright, his shoulders back, like a soldier awaiting the order to act. I marked him as a useful fellow.

Zaraband forced a gap through the throng, the men dodging to avoid her hooves.

I pointed my whip at the red-haired man.

"You! You know who I am. I am Lord Ambrose Malfine. Tell me what's going on here!"

The little man scrambled out from the shafts of the cart and stood before me with a kind of servility, yet looking aside, like the others.

"Look at me! Your name?"

The little man jerked his head and gazed straight up into my face. He was red-veined, a drinking man, a stalwart of the local tavern, I would guess, but controlled withal. His eyes closed and flickered for a moment when he looked at me, as I had seen in so many faces, but he held his gaze upon me steadily enough after that. I grudgingly gave him some respect for that. But it meant he was the more dangerous for it, a man not easily scared or intimidated.

"Seliman Day is my name, my lord, and I have no shame for my name. You can see here what has happened, plain as a pikestaff. That gypsy's killed 'em. Killed old Gideon Crawshay the farmer and his son, the both of them. Shot 'em in the farmhouse yonder. The gypsy were found with their money in his shirt in this very place. No use troubling to tek him to assizes. Finish him here—break him on the wheel. Thet'll teach 'em all—them thieves of gypsies."

He spat into the eyes of the bound man, who did not flinch or try to turn his face aside. He reminded me of a young bear I had seen on my travels, beaten, its claws and teeth drawn, made to leap with live coals, and then slumped with a terrible animal resignation to await whatever happened to it, all spirit broken, all hope gone. Where had I seen such a sight? Yes, in that hot country, a long time ago. The sickening smell of the beast's scorched pads, its blood and spittle, came like a flash of memory to taunt me.

Another man stepped forward.

"Aye, thet's what old Sir Anderton would hev done, my lord. He just let us hev 'em when 'twas gypsies like this 'un— said they ain't men, they comes out of nowhere, and they has nowhere and nothin'. We allus done what we liked to 'em. Them's vermin, like foxes and rats."

He waited for my acknowledgement, for my token of understanding that there was a clear difference between decent-living, respectable torturers such as Seliman Day and his cronies, and thieving ruffians like gypsies.

I did not hesitate. "Untie him!"

The red-haired man, Seliman Day, came forward, as if to protest. He would not dare to directly oppose me for I represented the greatest authority in a radius of a hundred miles, and disobedience to a member of the local gentry, even a strange specimen like myself, would be unthinkable. Sir Anderton Revers was the squire whose lands lay on the other side of the village, bordering with the grounds of Malfine for much of the way, and he was at present in London, as Belos had informed me, trying to find a suitor for his country blowsabella of a daughter, a Prince Florian who would lift the curse of the mortgage from the Revers estate. Lady Revers had given up any hope of me as a presentable candidate for her daughter's hand—even the prospect of money could not make the Revers desire to deliver up their plump little sacrificial lamb to the scarred and terrifying hermit of Malfine, for they had some natural parental feelings after all.

Sir Anderton was exactly the kind of country aristocrat these men understood. Heavy-drinking, capricious—had not opened a book these forty years. Sentenced them to be flogged or deported for petty theft, sent them a guinea at the birth of each of their brats and allowed them to live in tumbledown housing around his ill-managed estates. If he had been at home, they would have fetched him, he would have ridden away and let them do what they wanted to the gypsy, and a great deal of torment would have been saved thereby. Sir Anderton has, to put it mildly, no passionate urge for truth, and justice is a word that I do not think has ever figured in his vocabulary. He merely sits on the magistrate's bench and hands down sentences. That, for him, *is* justice.

And it may be that it would indeed have been the better course, to do as Sir Anderton would have done, to ride away and forget the incident altogether. The gypsy would be killed, as he no doubt richly deserved, and buried in some God-forsaken spot—no injustice there, for he was almost certainly not a Christian—and the family of the murdered men would be spared the prolonged ordeal of the trial. The county would be saved the expense of keeping the gypsy in prison and Sir Anderton would be saved the trouble of doing anything at all.

But I could not do this, I found. Somehow, in spite of all my resolutions, I was fool enough to get involved in humanity, there at Crawshay's farm, with idiotic scruples about finding evidence and observing the rule of law. The truth is that I had a sudden and unaccountable attack of the idealism which I had forsworn, that impulse that had once driven me to fight for the chimera called liberty. I thought it had been dead and buried long ago, buried in the sparse and rocky earth of Crete. Somehow, here, in this English setting, it sparked again from some hidden, banked-up embers, and kept me there, kept me between the cart and the crowd, to defend a man whose life was undoubtedly worthless.

"Untie him!" I said again. But Seliman pressed on. "My lord, this gypsy is a killer! Let us finish him now and save the King the trouble of trying and hanging."

There was a murmur of assent from the crowd, and they pushed in closer around my mare. Would they rebel against authority?

We in the south of England had not been much troubled by disorder among the people, although I knew there had been riots elsewhere in the country, especially in the factory towns of the north, where the weavers had been told to take wages lower even than the miserable pittance they were already receiving. Some had marched through the streets bearing black silk banners embroidered with sayings such as "We trust in God to bring us through," poor devils. And in the docks and alleyways of Bristol city the grievances of the poor shame the heavens, and must one day burst into riot. Riot, not revolution. Revolution is a word for other countries, where there is more hope of change.

In England today, God, of course, is on the side of the masters. The weavers might starve in the streets for aught any being, human or divine, would care. It is true that the mill-owners had a few frights—at Rochdale, new-fangled looms and spinning jennies which did the work so much faster and cheaper than human beings were smashed up by angry crowds. And there had been a touch of menace in a Macclesfield riot, where an angry crowd carried a pole with human teeth suspended from it, and a banner below the teeth bearing the words: "To let, the owners having no further use for them."

So elsewhere the local gentry had been threatened and magistrates had called out the militia, but here, far from Satanic textile mills or the hellish cotton factories, we had known peace and men lived as they had done for centuries, deferential, forelock-tugging. Our small country disorders, rarely more than tavern brawls, were easily quelled, and I had no fear of this mob at Crawshay's. I was not afraid of giving orders—had in fact held command over ruffians far more fierce than a bunch of farm hands, and I spoke out so that my voice would carry to all the group, including a few stragglers I saw at the back, men less certain than Seliman Day of their right to do what they would with the gypsy, especially now that there was someone to give orders. It is amazingly easy to command Englishmen: generally speaking, they have a longing for someone to take charge, they love to have authority over them, it makes them feel secure and they themselves need not trouble to think further. At least, that was my opinion, and it had this merit: that I had no fear of taking command of that rustic rabble.

But I needed an ally—one, at least.

I beckoned to the fellow who had stood aloof—an ex-soldier, if ever I saw one. He came forward.

"Name?"

I barked the word out in true military fashion, and got the automatic response of the well-drilled solider.

"Thomas Granby, sir . . . that is, my lord."

"Well, Granby, you have seen some service, I would say."

"I served King George, my lord."

Our eyes met. Men who have seen death on a battlefield share something in common, wherever they have fought.

"What regiment?"

"North Somersets, my lord."

Yellow facings on their red coats, silver lace—I had seen the North Somersetshire Infantry parading resplendently through Taunton, their recruiting sergeant luring just such country fellows as this to join them: to take the King's shilling and enter the antechambers of hell.

I saw that he had a clasp knife in his hand, held discreetly at his side. Would he use it for good or ill?

I took a chance.

"Granby, cut the prisoner free from the wheel and set him in the cart."

I turned to the assembled men.

"You know the law. The man is entitled to a trial."

Would the ex-soldier still prove obedient to orders? If he did not, he might well turn the balance against me.

There was a long pause.

Tom Granby stepped forward, raised his knife, and began to saw at the bonds.

There was an angry buzzing, curses uttered below the breath, from the men. Sir Anderton would have kept silent and let them have their way—of that they were well aware.

As for the cruelty of the death envisaged for this man, why, indeed it would teach those thieving gypsies to keep out of the county.

But just now authority in the county was represented not by the red-faced Anderton, familiar as the leading magistrate in these parts for some thirty years, but by myself, by the unreliable, shadowy and mysterious person of Lord Ambrose Malfine.

And authority was now ordering them to give up their prey.

Acceptance was ingrained, enforced by centuries of obedience to the local landowners and bowing their heads when a carriage swept by. They would do as I ordered. But I had to stare them down, raise my whip, edge Zaraband in a sideways dance towards the cart to get between the men and their wretched quarry.

My words were having some effect. A couple of the men were now pleading with the others to see reason; they were older, more sober heads. They knew the whole lot might hang on one gallows at the next assizes, because young Lord Ambrose did not see things in the same light as old Sir Anderton, and he might not turn a blind eye to what they did to their captive. Which would be, and even these country idiots knew it, one thing only. There was only one name for it.

Murder.

The ropes tying the gypsy to the wheel were cut through at last, and, on my orders, with kicks and curses, the men set the stranger up in the cart, tying him to the boards.

He was talking, calling out something, in a language they did not know, but which I could partly follow.

"I did not kill them. By God, I did not kill them."

And then, despairingly: *"Tatcho! Tatcho!"*

Which is to say, in their tongue, "It is truth! Truth!"

Why should he lie in the Romany language, which he thought none around him could understand?

One of the men was pulling at the stirrup of the bay.

"My lord, they are in the barn there. The men he killed."

CHAPTER 3

I dismounted and walked to the barn, the men following me.

The outhouse was stone-floored, whitewashed, clean. There were two trestle tables in the barn, and here, as if in an obscene parody of some farmhouse feast, lay the farmer, old Gideon Crawshay, and his handsome son Edmund, side by side in death.

As I drew closer to the bodies, the insects rose in a buzzing mass. Old Gideon was the nearer to the door. I saw what was left of the dead face, saw that the eyes were open and glaring, the teeth bared, the mouth in a fixed rictus. Was it an expression of rage? It seemed to me that it was of amazement rather; something had astounded old Crawshay at the very last, something that had left him with this incredulous glare upon his features as he died.

A big man, Gideon Crawshay, bushy-browed and full of hate. So he had been for most of his life and so he was in death.

I drew closer and peered over the body. Yes, old Crawshay's evil countenance agreed with all reports of his character in life; at any rate, until his recent supposed attack of virtue.

I had heard of this recent reformation of the old sot, a sudden conversion to civilised living; it was a titbit that Belos had reported to me a few months back, that old Crawshay the farmer had sobered up, got himself some fine clothes and dined at table like a human, the dirty old goat. Why or how this reformation had come about, the village did not know.

It made his death even more of a mystery. Old Gideon had frequently been fighting drunk when in his cups, and might have picked a quarrel with a saint: there must have been a score of men hereabouts whose ancestry, sexual powers and financial honesty had all been the subject of spirited abuse by the foul-mouthed old creature, but what had happened to him now did not fit with the image of a drunken brawl. I stepped further into the outhouse and closer to the body. To the bodies. Gideon and his son.

God help the coroner's jury when they came to view these corpses, I thought, for there was already a smell of putrescence in the air. The others had fallen back.

There were few men in England, unless perhaps they had gone the whole three days at Waterloo, who had seen what I had seen in the way of death. As it happened, I was the best person they could have sent for, since I have had very considerable experience of dealing with dead men in hot weather and do not puke at the smell.

I took mental note of what I saw. Crawshay had been killed by a bullet, probably from a pistol. And it had been fired at close range, tearing out half of his throat, a terrible wound from which the blood had gushed and dried in the heat to form an obscene brick-coloured cravat, a velvety crust of blood that spilled over his breast, vivid against the handsome white linen of his shirt, starched and ruffled.

On the other table, a long form with the head hanging down over one end, fair hair trailing in the dust. Crawshay's son, Edmund. His heir.

But not, so village gossip had it, his pride and joy. Crawshay had openly despised his son, and I remembered fragments of grown-up conversations in whispering rooms, things I had overheard but not understood, as a child, before I had gone away, tittle-tattle about the Crawshays passing round the village from one clacking tongue to another. Edmund had not resembled his father at all, except that now he had shared the manner of his death. He had the light gold hair, the wistful good looks of his long-dead mother. And he had her softness.

Here now they lay, father and son, side by side, and the blond hair that women had thought so attractive and Crawshay had sneered at so often was darkened with blood, and handsome Edmund was handsome no longer because a bullet had carried away the side of his face and his jaw was smashed to white fragments of bone, and his beautiful even white teeth were blown to stumps.

Seliman Day was behind me, the only one of the village men to have come into the barn. He had a cloth bundle in one fist. "My lord, they was shot inside the house—that's where we found 'em. But Mistress Crawshay, she were making such a hollering and weeping, we brought them out and laid them here, and she were calmer then. And then she told us about the gypsy-man, and we caught 'un straight away. He must hev been making for that caravan of theirs when we git him. He were carrying this. Caught red-handed, and thet's the truth."

He handed the bundle to me and I unwrapped it in silence. In my hands lay some fine white linen with tiny smocking—a child's shirt, perhaps—with reddish-brown smears upon it. And inside that, something heavy and gleaming—half a dozen gold guineas fell out into my palm, and there was a big old-fashioned silver watch, the kind which is so appropriately called a "turnip," such as farmers have. It had dark, dry smears on it, dulling its brightness as I held it up to the light.

"That's his watch. That's old Crawshay's watch. He were an evil old bastard, Crawshay, and I'll say that even over his dead body. But bin murdered here like a beast, and he were one of us, and shall us see his killer here and do nowt?"

He had only to call on the men outside and it was still
possible they would break the frail bounds of obedience that
contained their lust for revenge, their feverish, almost sexual excitement at the prospect of seeing the gypsy's physical
agony. And they might not stop at the gypsy. If I tried to
come between them and their prey and they were in a truly
murderous mood of self-righteous revenge, why, then Lord
Ambrose and the gypsy both might go the same way to a
hideous death at the hands of a mob. Danger was screaming
through the stench and the heat. But something told me the
greater danger would be to back down now, to lose my stance
of authority. Once I showed any sign of fear, once they
sensed for an instant that I was not their master, they would
be out of control.

I stepped outside the barn. There was a menacing little
crowd still gathered around. But the gypsy had been freed
from the wheel of the cart. They had obeyed me in that, at
least—it was a good sign.

"This bundle here is evidence for a warrant and one will
be issued as soon as I get back. The gypsy is to be taken to
Malfine and locked away in the cellars. We'll get him to
Callerton Assizes and then he'll swing in the end—if he's
guilty. But you must leave it to judge and jury. You know
the consequences otherwise—I cannot protect you from the
results of any wrongdoing you commit. You all know that.
Now step back and do as I tell you! Step back, I say!"

There was some murmuring, but a kind of grudging assent to what I had said. There were hotheads here, but not
fools. They would obey me. I could tell when a man would
be obeyed and when he would not.

I walked outside and over to the cart where the Romany
lay lashed down inside it, like a beast trussed for market. I
climbed up and looked down into his dark eyes and I could
read nothing there—not guilt, not even fear. There was an
animal sense of danger, a foxy alertness in his body, rather
than human knowledge. But it might have been the smell

coming from him, a sour, piss-drenched stink, that put me in mind of a fox.

"Take him to Malfine and hold him there till I come," I said. "You, Day—and you—Granby, is it?"

I pointed at the ex-soldier, the man who had cut the gypsy from the wheel in response to my orders.

"Aye, my lord."

"Well, you two, Day and Granby, you are responsible for the safety of this man, d'you hear? I want him in one piece when I get back to Malfine. You'll hang for it otherwise. I'll not have the law flouted here!"

That should keep the gypsy safe for the moment. Those two knew I had their names, knew they would be held responsible for what happened. Granby had some ingrained discipline and training, and Seliman Day could clearly have some influence on a crowd—I hoped he would now use it for the good, that is to say, to protect his own skin. Those two would swing their weight against a lynching party.

I don't know why I was so concerned with the fate of the gypsy. Why didn't I leave the wretch to be dealt with then and there? No one would have bothered about it, even if the outside world had ever heard of his untimely demise.

I could have turned my back. I could have walked away. Certainly, I felt nothing about the creature. Or had there been something, when I looked into his eyes? A kind of movement within my mind, as if something were opening, slightly, like the cage of an animal feared by its keeper?

I knew what to do with the bodies, and it must be done immediately. They could not receive burial, for the coroner's jury must see them. But they could not lie here—I knew only too well what happened to men's bodies in such heat. Stinking carrion within a few hours.

The Malfine icehouse, like most of the other architectural delights and follies on the estate that had been built to accommodate a semi-palatial lifestyle, had not been used for a quarter of a century, but it was partly underground, chilled by a running stream, and furnished with cold marble benches. Two of those would make fitting biers for the Crawshays in this heat.

"Day, where is Mistress Crawshay? I'll have to talk to her. Mistress Edmund Crawshay, is it not?"

"Aye, my lord. The old 'un had no wife—leastways, not yet, though some do say he had intentions that way. But 'tis Mistress Edmund runs the 'ouse, and she were in a terrible state when we come, but she's calmed down a bit by now. She were crying and shrieking something terrible, but 'tis all quiet now. There's a wumman with 'er. The governess is taking care of her."

CHAPTER 4

❧

"GO to the farmhouse. Tell them I am coming."

Granby advanced in long strides to the looming doorway. His lanky form moved up the shadowless path.

At least the women could be forewarned. I waited for a few minutes, gazing round at the dilapidated outhouses of the farm, and then walked up to the front of the house. The long barrow known as Wayland's Mound rose behind it. It made the house darker, but I suppose old Gideon had never thought to have it levelled.

It was a big house for a local farmer. The Crawshays had once been respected in these parts, and they had been wealthy enough to live in what was considerable style in a farming community. But in the last century, as the fortunes of my family, the Malfines, increased, those of the Crawshays had been on the wane. There had been still some lingering style about the old man; he had been well schooled, capable of a certain grace, between and sometimes even during his bouts of drunkenness, though he had been shunned by his neighbours for many years.

The heavy oak door of the farmhouse was standing open

and I stepped inside, into a stone passage. My eyes adjusted
to the dimness, and I felt the cold of the flagstones striking
up, even on this hot day. There was another door, leading off
the passage to the left. I knocked perfunctorily upon it and
walked into a low, long room. A parlour, by its furnishings.

Perhaps they had seen me from the window. At any rate,
they did not seem to be surprised. I even had the impression
that they were waiting for me, that they had formed a tableau
for my entrance.

One woman was standing near the window. The other was
slumped in a chair by the door. The woman near the window
looked directly at me as I entered.

The parlour had some unexpectedly graceful furnishings.
There were several fine old pieces of furniture, such as a delicate little walnut armchair. Heavy curtains of that rose-gilt
colour that used to be called old gold, in watered silk. And
something rarely seen in the house of a farmer, however prosperous: a pretty cottage piano, with an embroidered Indian
shawl thrown over the top.

I had to stoop because of the low ceiling.

The woman standing near the window on the other side of
the room was outlined against the light. She was strong and
tall, with a mass of chestnut hair piled on her neck. A handsome woman. Handsome, rather than beautiful, was what
they would say of her. Nothing fragile. "Nothing fancy to look
at," as they say in these parts.

Nothing fancy.

Except for the eyes.

As she turned her head at my approach, the light fell on
her face, and I saw that the governess's eyes were of a most
strange colour, a smoky yellowish-grey, light eyes, set perhaps a trifle too close together, giving her face a secret look.

That blankness, that impassivity, was so unexpected it
was almost shocking in itself.

This, I knew, was Miss Anstruther, the recently arrived
governess to the Crawshay child. The pretension of having
a governess for a farmer's family was something that had

not escaped mocking comment. So busy had the wagging
tongues been that I believe Miss Anstruther must have been
the subject of almost as much gossip as I myself. We two
were the outsiders in this place—we still had novelty value.
Whisper, whisper, whisper:

"They say he bought her, my lord! Old Gideon Crawshay,
at the farm. He bought a governess at Callerton Fair."

I could just imagine the excitement in the district, the
chattering tongues, the mittened hands of the ladies waving
in excitement in the drawing rooms, the lips of the farmers
slopping warm piss-ale in the village inn. "*Bought* her, they
say! Fancy that! And what do you suppose he paid for her?
Nobody knows!"

Outside, a cloud must have passed from the sun, for a flood
of light suddenly fell through the window and I saw that
there was a great stain across the front of the governess's modest dove-grey velvet dress. It was a broad brownish smear.
Dried blood.

She has touched the bodies and not changed her gown, I
thought. The other woman had not the slightest stain on her,
although her skirts seemed draggled and dusty. But her hair
was combed neatly and pulled over her ears, parted down the
centre, and her sleek ringlets fell on either side of her pale
face. Her dress was of sprigged cotton, little blue florets on a
cream ground, tight across her breasts. She had a hand over
her face.

Strange that the governess had a richer gown than her mistress. Marie Crawshay's day-dress, pretty though it was, was
simple and ordinary, rather like that of a maid in a well-to-do
household. The governess's gown, on the other hand, though
plain, was of the finest lustrous Italian silk velvet—in fact, it
was of the same quality as my own frock-coats, which was
why I recognised it for what it was.

I advanced into the room. Marie, Edmund's widow, had
taken her hand away from her face and was staring at me. She
licked her upper lip, slowly, like an animal. A faint smell of
sweat, mingled with that of cologne, arose from her body.

The woman was drugged.

The iris of her deep-blue eye was glassy, the pupil reduced, the skin clammy and yellowish. I knew those signs, had seen them before in the feverish context of a military hospital: Mistress Edmund Crawshay had been calmed by laudanum, that is, by opium admixed with brandy. I know not why laudanum is believed to be such a harmless remedy that even nurses give it to fretful children to soothe their teething: I myself, in my fighting campaigns, had seen its operation often enough in the makeshift camps where the wounded and diseased were nursed, and observed that it gave much relief from pain and fever, but that men had then to be weaned from it if they were not to become mostly wretchedly addicted to its use, as poor Tom De Quincey has described in his *Confessions*.

This condition that I now saw in Mistress Crawshay at the farmhouse was, I knew, an unnatural tranquillity, the peace of the poppy, the two-edged, untrustworthy, merciful release given by opium, the blissful calm that might break into hysteria at any moment.

"Madam, my condolences."

There was a slight nod in return. The lace handkerchief dabbed at the eyes.

Pretty eyes, big and blue, with dark lashes, repeated in the small, solemn face of her son, who was clutching at her skirt, staring up at me in silence. The child had the golden hair of his father who now lay in death outside these walls, on a trestle table not ten yards away, those same thick yellow curls that I had seen darkened and dabbled with blood in the outhouse.

A handsome family, the Crawshays, and no doubt, like so many families where beauty is the general run of the mill and the expected inheritance, intolerant of physical defects.

"Madam, I am Ambrose Malfine, your neighbour, and, I hope, your friend. They have sent for me because Sir Anderton is away and someone must needs take charge here. I hesitate to press you, but there are questions that must be asked, and it is better that I should put them to you now than that you should be exposed to questioning before the coroner's jury."

I knew something of the law in such cases. She would have to make a formal deposition at some stage, since she was probably the chief witness to the guilt of the gypsy. And she would have to give evidence at his trial. They would hang him in the end, of course, no doubt about that. If she could give me her account of events now, that would be enough to send him for trial and the formalities could follow later. The rope would encircle his neck in the fullness of time.

"Mistress Crawshay, will you not tell me what passed here this morning?"

Marie Crawshay turned to the governess. She licked her lips with a small red tongue, opening her mouth silently several times, as if she could not get the words out, but finally managed: "Please take my son out of the room."

Miss Anstruther detached the little fingers from Marie's skirts and with surprising strength gathered the child up easily in her arms and carried him out of the room. He made no protest. Marie Crawshay waved me to a chair and sank back, falling giddily into a pile of velvet cushions.

"I tried to keep my son away from what happened here, but of course, I couldn't hide everything . . ."

Marie's voice faltered and she twisted her hands tightly in her lap.

"Shall I tell you what I saw, my lord? Now? Well, I was alone when it happened. Miss Anstruther—my governess—had gone—had gone on some . . . some errands for me, to Callerton. The farm hands were all out in the fields. Edmund, my husband . . ."

Her eyes filled with tears, and they ran down her delicate pink cheeks and fell in little damp patches on to the lace at her neck, but she carried on.

"I heard a noise. A bang. I had my son with me—we were in the barn across the yard. He has a favourite little calf, all of his own—Primrose—and when she is older she will give milk just for him, so I told him. He likes to see her every morning—he runs across the yard to pet her."

Dear God, I thought, what must old Crawshay have thought of that? A working farm, and the indulgent fancy of a cow kept just as a pet for the child!

"There will be a trial, will there not? Will I have to testify? In court?"

"Your evidence will be needed, Mistress Crawshay. I fear we cannot spare you that."

"No, no, I understand . . . If I tell you now, just quietly . . . with only the two of us here, perhaps I will be less frightened when it comes to the courtroom."

Cool. She was very cool. There was a pulse beating very slowly in her throat. It was the drug.

"Well then, yesterday afternoon . . . Shall I start there? It was so hot . . . I think it must be the hottest summer . . .

"I was in the dairy when it happened. We had all had our dinner at noon. Then Miss Anstruther left in the pony and trap for Callerton. She was going to do some shopping there. My husband and . . . Crawshay—they always called him just Crawshay in the village, just his surname—they were doing accounts in the dining room here. I left them at the long dinner table. The dishes had been cleared away and they had the farm account books spread out in front of them. I did a few necessary things in the kitchen, wrapping the ham in muslin and that kind of thing. Then I went out to the dairy. That barn . . . that place where they are now . . . that was the old dairy at one time, but it hasn't been used as a dairy for a century or more, I think, because Crawshay's great-grandfather had another one built . . . I mean, the one we use now. I'm so sorry, my lord, my mind wanders from the point, I know. Please forgive me. Anyway, I had tasks to do in the dairy. It was so hot the milk has been tainting quickly. Mattie, that's our servant, Mattie had gone home to the village. She does not always scour out all the pans properly and I wanted to scald them myself with boiling water, to make them sweet. I went to the dairy and I took Edmund with me. He brought his little wooden horse and he played quietly with that while I was at work. He's a sweet-natured boy, you know. He was pretending to churn butter for me. Crawshay thought my boy was too gentle, he wanted to make him a bit more of a rapscallion, that's what he used to say, a rapscallion. We were in the dairy for the best part of the afternoon. I gave Edmund a drink of milk there, warm from the cow. And Edmund had his arms about his calf and he was petting her and stroking her—when I heard a couple of loud bangs from the direction of the house."

She stopped short.

Was it real shock? Marie Crawshay might seem a shrinking flower, but she was a farmer's wife. She would be used to the sound of gunshots—popping off at rabbits and hares, perhaps after bigger game in my own woods, for I could not be bothered to do anything about the poaching that took place in the grounds of Malfine at night.

"Did you know they were shots?"

"Yes, but I thought nothing of it. I thought someone was shooting a coney, or some such little creature. But then I heard another, and then I was quite certain—certain that shots had come from the house. So then I knew of course, it was all wrong. It wasn't someone out in the fields. I told Edmund to stay with the calf—he's such a good child, you know. And then I ran out of the dairy. But I didn't run straight to the house. I don't know why, perhaps something . . . some instinct . . . I must have sensed something because I didn't run straight across the yard. Lord Ambrose, perhaps God watches over us sometimes."

Well, yes, and then again, perhaps He doesn't, I thought. He hadn't done much watching over her husband and her father-in-law.

"I was very frightened, you see, so I didn't run in straight away—crept up, keeping close to the wall. The door to the house was open and I stood just inside it—and something saved me, something kept me from crying out. Because he was still there, you see, the murderer. Just the other side of that wall.

"And as I stood there listening just inside the front door, I heard nothing. Absolutely nothing. And that was wrong, you see. The silence was wrong. Because the old man, my father-in-law, Mr. Crawshay—he was not a silent man. I was expecting to hear something: Edmund and old Crawshay talking, or even arguing, but there was nothing at all. There should have been some sounds, even just the noises of them moving around the room—you know, there are sounds in a room even when people aren't talking.

"But there was just that dreadful silence, and I stepped a little further down the passage, and then I smelled a bitter, burning scent, and I knew what it was, the smell of gunpowder. And the dining room door, the door at the end of the passage, was open a crack. So I crept up to it. I held my breath. And then I did hear something. I heard someone moving, but with little creeping movements like my own.

"I put my eye to the crack of the door. And I saw him. The gypsy. Bending over something on the floor. Then he moved, and I could see what it was lying there."

She stopped suddenly, and gripped the arms of the chair so tightly that I could see the blue veins swelling up under the pale knuckles. A look of terror crossed her face. "He's not here now, is he? You've taken him away? Say you've taken him away!"

There was a decanter with little gilded glasses beside it on a round table near the window. I took out the stopper and sniffed at it. Wine. I poured out a glass and held it to her lips; I put my arm around her thin, shaking shoulders.

She swallowed the drink in little shuddering sips. Slowly, her hands relaxed their grip on the arms of her chair and the shuddering ceased.

"Now listen to me, Mistress Crawshay. You mean the gypsy, don't you? The gypsy frightens you. We've taken him away. He can never hurt you again. You're quite safe now, quite safe."

Whether it was the wine, or my reassurances, she seemed able to go on.

"You can't stay forever in a nightmare, can you?" she said forlornly. "You must wake up some time!"

Then she was speaking again, fast and determined, with a sudden access of strength.

"Before I tell you any more, you must tell me something. Tell me where the gypsy is now. I have the right to know!"

"I'll give orders to have him locked up. He'll be in the cellar of my house, five miles away. Guarded by two men; deep underground at Malfine, with a padlock and iron bolts on the door of his prison. There's no escape for him—I give you my word on that."

Marie gazed at me for a few moments, as if testing me for honesty. Then she turned her head away and began to talk again.

"You'll want to know what I saw. It was the gypsy. He was holding one of the pistols, bending over something on the floor, and then he moved and I saw them.

"I saw Edmund first. I could see Edmund's hair, and blood everywhere, and that devil bending over him, and he turned his wicked face towards the door and he seemed to be looking straight at me, and I was afraid he could see me, even through the wood of the door—you know what they say in the village, that the gypsies have the second sight, that they can see through solid walls! He seemed to be looking right at me, but then I saw that he was staring at something—something he was holding up in his hand. It caught the light and I could see what it was. It was the old man's silver fob watch—I would have known it anywhere.

"I knew then that I had to get away. I was certain he would kill me if he saw me. For I knew he must have killed them both, Edmund and old Crawshay. The old man would never have let the watch go—he had it always on a chain.

I was afraid of everything when I saw that watch in the hand of the gypsy.

"I was afraid that I could not trust my feet, that they would not move, that I would cry out, that the door would creak, that I would faint. But I thought of my boy! I had to get my child away from the farm and safe from that devil! And eventually I forced my legs to carry me, creeping along, back out of the house. It seemed years before I got down that passageway, tiptoeing, a step at a time. Still no sound from the dining room. Then I slipped outside and into the byre and held little Edmund tight, and put my hand across his mouth in case he cried out, and we crouched down in the straw. At last I heard the outer gate of the farmyard creaking, and I stood up and peered out and I saw him—the gypsy—running down the lane.

"I told little Edmund to stay there in the straw and not to make a sound. And I went back to the house. They were there—in the dining room. My husband and his father."

CHAPTER 5

THEFT was almost certainly the motive—at least for the beginning of the crime which had ended in a double murder. It would be death to be convicted of this robbery alone, and if the wretched gypsy had been caught in the act of theft by the Crawshays, father and son, he might as well have murdered them. After all, he could only be hanged once. He would have nothing to lose by killing them.

"Mistress Crawshay, please help me. Calm yourself and answer me. Was any money missing?"

"They might have had some money there. They were doing the accounts for the farm tenants, and some of them had paid their rents recently. The old man and my husband might have been counting up the rents. And the watch is missing, of course. The fob watch the gypsy ran off with. And something else—something that seems very strange, although I didn't notice it had gone until a little while ago. A bundle of old clothes—quite worthless, really. Why should he take that? Why should he take some old linen? I had put a few things on a side table, ready to be mended. Just some old shirts and some little kerchiefs, for my son. The bundle is missing. Why should he take that? I would have given it to him if he had begged it from me—I was never ungenerous—anyone in the village would tell you that."

Why had he taken the linen? I guessed, but I could not tell Marie. To wipe the blood of his victims from his hands. If he had stolen the watch from Crawshay, he must have had to dabble in the old man's blood in order to reach into his pocket, where the watch would be fastened. Better not be mentioned now.

Marie seemed exhausted. She lay back and closed her eyes. I had to ask her one more question.

"The weapon. Where did it come from?"

She spoke with her eyes closed, but clearly.

"Weapons. It was a brace of pistols. I believe they had both been fired. They were on the dresser."

That explained the speed of the killings, and why the murderer had not needed to reload between shots. Little knowledge of firearms had been needed, therefore. Only the cold-blooded ability to hold the pistol steady, aim it at another human being and pull the trigger. And when that fellow creature had exploded into blood and torn flesh, the determination to repeat the act.

Marie was speaking again.

"My husband had been cleaning the pistols. They were an old pair, never used, as I remember. I think they've been in the family for a long time. Edmund took it into his head to clean them up—I expect he loaded them then. He had left them on the dresser in the dining room. He should have put them away, shouldn't he, and not left them loaded? He made thing easy for his murderer. Poor Edmund—he always made things easy for everyone!"

Was there a flicker of contempt in her voice? If there had been, it passed and she lapsed into silence, breathing in harsh gasps.

In that English farmhouse, I stood in the August heat and recalled myself as I had once been—young, glowing for liberty, ready to use all my powers in its cause—ready even to die for it, as Tom Granby had doubtless been ready to die for his King. Young men don't know what death is like. They think, they are taught, that it is glamorous and beautiful, a noble crown for heroes to seek out, a painless martyrdom, achieved without suffering. Heroes have no blood, no sordid guts, no bones to splinter, no bowels to burst and leak.

The deaths I had seen in war were as dirty and squalid as those at home—worse, even, than what I had seen today, the stolid farmers with their blood and brains scattered over the trestle tables where they lay like butchered animals.

The gypsy had committed the murders, almost certainly. Almost.

But what if he had not?

If he was innocent—and Marie had not, even by her own drug-fevered account, seen him actually pull the trigger—then someone else had killed Edmund Crawshay and his father, here in this house.

And that someone was still at liberty.

I would make sure that young Granby was posted here tonight. He seemed one of the more reliable of the local turnips—a brawny, sunburned lad, not too bright, but sensible enough.

I had never been inside Crawshay's before, but I was able to guess the layout of the farmhouse. The passage, barred by doors at either end, allowed access from the lane that ran along one side of the house, and from the farmyard at the other side. Beasts and muddy loads could thus be taken right through the house along the passageway, without dirtying or disturbing the household.

The parlour had probably once, a couple of centuries before, been a cattle pen, when humans and animals lived under the same roof in wintry weather, huddled up for warmth, their breath and body heat mingling in the smoke from the hearth. Later Crawshays had added refinements, the beasts had been excluded to stand dumbly in their sheds outside, and now the farm boasted a smart parlour fit for ladies to sit in. On the side of the passage opposite the parlour was the principal room, which had once been the great hall of the farmhouse: I pushed open the door and walked into it, gazing round in the dusty sunlight. Here Crawshay had held to the old ways. There was a great fireplace at one end, where the cooking for the whole household must still be done, in the traditional way. There was a huge and tunnel-like bread oven built into the thickness of the wall at one side of the fireplace, and beside it stood the long-handled rakes and shovels with which the loaves were put in at the back of the oven, and pulled out when they were cooked, too hot for the touch. A tripod hung over the empty grate basket in the fireplace. They would not have been making fires and eating hot food in this weather, but bread would still be baked, and the fire would probably be lit once a week for that purpose, even in summer. The arrangements were such as could have been seen in country houses three centuries ago; even for this remote place, in the depths of the countryside, they would be considered very old-fashioned.

I took my time and moved away from the bread oven with reluctance—it had suddenly stirred a memory of sweet fragments of warm milk-bread, newly baked, handed to a drowsy child cradled on a nurse's lap.

On the other side of the fireplace was a small staircase, closed at the bottom by a door, which would lead up behind the chimney stack to the bedrooms. This, too, was an old arrangement I was familiar with in the houses hereabouts. Once this would have been the only staircase. A grand wide staircase sweeping up from the entrance hall was often added later on, when a bit more grace and show were called for. The Crawshays had not thought it worth their while.

A huge dining table had been placed, not in the middle of the room, but close enough to the fire to get its warmth in winter. This was where they had been seated, Crawshay and his son, at the table, near the empty grate, and this was where they had died. It was probably in all innocence that the bodies had been removed to an outhouse, to spare Marie Crawshay the ghastly thought that the men of her family were left sprawled in an ugly death, lying as they had fallen, in the next room, but it meant I had to reconstruct what had happened here from the traces that were left.

There were deep stains on the wood of the table. They would never get them out of the unvarnished old timber. They might scrub the table with lye, with silver sand, but already the blood had soaked deeply into the grain, as I could see. The blood had sprayed out, splashing the walls, and had formed two pools, one very heavy, at the end of the table nearest the door that led into the passage. The most blood was in front of a great carver chair, the kind used by the master of the house, and traditionally reserved for him alone. The other stain was smaller and less blood had soaked into the wood, but underneath the table there were black clots of it still, in the rushes that were strewn on the floor in the old-fashioned way. Probably they had not yet been noticed, and the rushes would eventually be cleared from the stone-flagged floor. Very few people used them nowadays, but Crawshay must have been a tyrant in insisting on the old country ways.

I could picture the scene now. The old man, old Crawshay, with his shock of white hair and his angry jowls, seated facing the door as the killer entered from the passageway. The murderer had perhaps not expected to find the two men at home at all—they were usually out on the farm for most of the day, and now, at harvest-time, every available creature would be needed in the fields, even such a delicate animal as Edmund Crawshay. If the Crawshays had not been doing the accounts, they would not have been here in the house at all.

I moved around the table, trying this way and that, trying out how the two men had sat, trying to see what they had seen.

Old Crawshay had been here, at the head of the table, facing the door as the killer entered. Edmund had sat at the side, not facing his father. They had slumped forward after the shots, and the blood had collected in pools beneath their heads.

And what of the weapons? Yes, just inside the door. There was a dresser against a side wall and on it a cleaning rod and some oily rags. Helpful Edmund, as Marie had said, cleaning the pistols ready for use.

Someone had retrieved the pistols after the murder, and put them carefully back on the dresser, side by side. I lifted one, weighed it in my hand, turned it over. It was a beautiful piece of workmanship. The pistols, a matched pair, were duelling weapons, a splendid brace, made with a skill and elegance that could scarcely be surpassed. I looked closely at the steel damascening and the chased silver butts.

I put the pistols down, and concentrated on what had happened in that room. Probably, no one would ever know all the details. But the gypsy had come to the house—it was his habit to do so, old Seliman had told me, to come every day. The gypsy was helping out in the fields during the harvest, and though he was not fed with the other labourers at the end of the day, Marie usually gave him a pitcher of milk or some cider and a bit of bread to take with him. But on this occasion, Marie, according to her story of events, had been out in the dairy with her son. So the gypsy had pushed open the door, unlocked as always, and stepped along the passage. He had no business to do so, of course. And perhaps Crawshay had heard his footfalls; perhaps he had flung out a challenge, called out suspiciously at the sound of the movement outside the room.

And then, if the gypsy had even been accused of theft, two such substantial witnesses as a stout local farmer and his son would be enough to get the man convicted at the next assizes, and hanged as speedily thereafter as might be managed.

So when the man realised what such an accusation would mean, that he would inevitably hang from a gallows tree, when he looked around and saw the pistols, bright and gleaming after Edmund had cleaned them, it was the work of a second to reach for them and point them at his accuser. And then the work of a few moments to fire, perhaps at old

Crawshay as he was still in the act of rising from his chair and calling out his accusation, and at his son, Edmund, there by his side. Now I understood that vicious amazement on the dead man's face, I thought to myself, that look fixed there until the flesh itself should decay, an appearance of surprise and shock, rather than fear, the look of one who has seen a black beetle turn on him as he is about to crush it.

The gypsy fired a pistol, and the ball caught Crawshay full in the throat. He pitched forward, and his life's blood ran out.

And then there was Edmund. He would have had no time for thought—just moments enough perhaps to turn and look with horror at his assailant, before the second pistol exploded death and the gypsy fired at Edmund's innocent head, blasting through the side of his skull.

Yes, that, or something very like it, was what had happened in this room.

I had arrangements to make about Crawshays recently deceased, and could not spend time speculating about their ancestors. Yet the atmosphere of the house, the plain solidity of its origins, the tradition of honest labour and simple pleasure which it exuded, was working away at something in my mind. Perhaps it was a long-buried affection and attachment to a country I had come to despise, perhaps a return to some things, stolid, solid English things, certain plain and strong realities, the hard surfaces of wood roughly planed by some local carpenter, the dark, secure roof beams, the clean-cut grey stone. These stable, stuffy, hard-edged traditions of farmhouse living found some chord within me, struck deep down at some old notes, some rough country music, some feeling for the land around me that I had not experienced since my return from the wild, hot shores of Greece.

I went back into the hall; there must be, besides the rooms I had already seen, quarters for work and storage. I found a passage that led to a series of work rooms, stone-flagged like the hall and passageway, cool even in this weather. There was a huge walk-in larder with marble slabs for shelves, and flitches of bacon, wrapped in muslin, hanging from hooks in the ceiling. The window was covered with a fine mesh against flies. And there was a still room, with nothing much left on its shelves, a few jars of jellies and preserved fruit, the labels peeling off and difficult to read.

Beyond was proof that Marie Crawshay's marriage had brought her to hard labour. There was a washhouse next to the still room, with tubs and wooden scrubbing-boards, and, the only modern note, an iron boiler with a stove grate to heat the water. There was a servant, Mattie, who came in from the village, I recalled, so perhaps she had done some of the heavy work here, but there were piles of linen waiting to be washed, both coarse rough farm shirts and smocks and some fine ruffled shirts. Marie, as she was at present, shocked and weeping, looked as if she could scarcely have lifted the pile of linen, in those thin, blue-veined arms.

Curious. There was a faint warmth coming from the wood-burning stove that heated the boiler. I picked up a pair of tongs that lay nearby and lifted the lid of the stove. Inside was a pile of ash, and over the bars that would have contained the logs were some silvery splashes, as if something molten had dropped on to them.

I made nothing of them at the time. I raked through the ashes, idly. There were some fragments of cloth, blackened, but with a small, neat pattern still faintly visible upon them.

The passage from the front door ran straight through the house. The door at the other end, into the farmyard, had massive bolts on it. They were secure. I checked them carefully. There were only the two entrances, front and back.

I walked back along the passage and stepped outside the front door of the farmhouse. Enough of these cloddish farmers and their history.

The gypsy had done it. That was a certainty. Yet there was a faint shadow of doubt. Marie had not actually seen him fire the shots. If I were to make the supposition that he had not committed the crimes—in short, if I were to treat him as the law says we must treat a man who has not yet been tried, that is, as if he were innocent till proven guilty . . . if he had not done it?

If the gypsy was innocent, then the real murderer was roaming free.

And if the real murderer suspected that Marie Crawshay had seen him? Or even the child—the child might have seen something. In that case, their lives would not be worth a silver pin.

Tom Granby was waiting outside. The crowd of men had dispersed, and he stood alone, his face ruddy in the hot sunshine, waiting patiently, as soldiers wait for orders.

"Where did you serve, Tom?"

"In France, my lord. I went as a drummer-boy and served for fifteen year, all told, till we was disbanded wi' the peace and all."

"And what do you now? Do you have a trade?"

"I'm a carpenter, my lord, but there's little work hereabouts."

I was not truly concerned with his occupation, but rather satisfying myself as to whether I had a disciplined and solid fellow whom I might make my lieutenant, as it were. Tom Granby was good enough.

"Tom, I want you to spend the night here. You are to make sure there is no attempt to enter the farmhouse, do you understand? You will make up some sort of bed in the passage inside the door of the farmhouse. The only other entrance is at the back and it's securely bolted. I'll send a rifle and some ammunition over from the gun room at Malfine. There's some smoked ham in the dairy—cut yourself a slice or two for your supper. As for Mistress Crawshay—Mistress Crawshay is not to be disturbed. If you need anything, call for the governess, Miss Anstruther."

I was puzzled about something.

"Tom, how came the alarm to be raised? How did you know in the village? It's three miles or more from the farm."

"The governess—Miss Anstruther—she had just come back with the cart from Callerton. She said she had just

turned into the yard when Mistress Crawshay started hollering and screaming inside the house. So Miss Anstruther, she
leaps up in the cart again, whips up the old pony, and down
to the village with the news. I were first in through the door
when we got here."

"Did you see the gypsy?"

"Nay, but Mistress Crawshay were yelling and screaming
as how the gypsy-man had done it—killed them Crawshays,
both of them, and run off beyond the house. So some of us
makes after him, like, and finds him just along the road there,
same as old Seliman said."

"Mistress Crawshay—did you see any blood on her
gown? Had she touched them?"

"I didn't see no speck of blood on her. Miss Anstruther,
she had a great smear of blood across her gown, I saw that
all right, but she said how she'd bent over old Crawshay and
tried to lift his head up—and then she saw as how he'd been
shot in the neck. But Mistress Crawshay, she were as clean as
a whistle. Not a speck of blood anywhere. Reckon she must
have kept well clear of them."

I suddenly felt desperately tired; the great newly healed
scar across my body began to throb. This English countryside was my retreat from that cruel, stony land in which I
had recently fought: this should have been my green, secured and ordered hermitage. And yet it had turned into
this parched and murderous terrain. The stench of the dead,
the blood, the laudanum-drugged woman—these had no
place here . . .

Yet they were not delusions, but horribly real enough,
though death and tragedy did not belong here in this stolid
English farmhouse, and neither did I. The wounded animal,
myself, needed peace to nurse its scars, to get to my own
ground, to my den, my lair, if you like to call it, within the
encircling walls of the mansion of Malfine.

"Tom, help get the bodies moved from here to the icehouse at Malfine."

Tom gave a dry laugh.

"I reckon that's the only place for them in this hot weather, my lord. Your worship won't be fancying any cold drinks for a while, though."

I drew a half-sovereign out of my pocket and gave it to Tom.

"Get yourself a bottle of brandy. You'll need some for this work."

Zaraband was tethered outside the farmhouse. I swung into the saddle, she danced for a moment to show me her paces, and then I turned her head for Malfine.

CHAPTER 6

WHEN I returned from Crawshay's after my encounters
with the living and the dead, I stepped gratefully into the
cool hall of Malfine. Belos brought me a glass of hock.
There was no ice, of course: as I said, the icehouse that
would serve as a temporary tomb for the Crawshay men had
been unused for many a year. Belos, who did not stand on
his dignity as butler, because I gave him no chance to do so,
helped me off with my boots and brought the hock with his
usual diplomatic anticipatory speed.

"Belos, have you heard the news?"

He had, from the men who came with the gypsy in the
cart.

"But if the gypsy is not guilty, my lord . . ."

"My own thought exactly, Belos. If the gypsy is innocent,
then who is guilty? Have you heard anything in the village—
any gossip in the alehouse? It seemed to me that the little fellow, Seliman Day, that he was keen enough to set the blame
on the Romany. Was there any quarrel between him and the
Crawshays?"

"I have heard nothing of that nature, my lord—the

Crawshays were not loved in the village, to say the least of it, but they kept pretty much to themselves—and I know of no quarrel with Day, nor with any of the villagers, come to that."

"Perhaps the gypsy *is* guilty," said I. "Or perhaps this matter will never be resolved."

" 'It will have blood, they say; blood will have blood.' "

"*Macbeth,* I believe, Belos—oh, forgive me!"

I had forgotten that theatrical folk count it the most unlucky thing in the world to mention the title of that work, an odd superstition, but one which Belos adheres to, though God knows he quotes from the Scottish play often enough, and so I told him.

"You quote too much literature for a member of the lower orders, Belos. Have I not told you so before?"

"Yes, my lord, but you will pardon a broken-down actor."

"And that you were when I found you penniless in Greece, Belos, but you tread the boards no longer. Kindly confine your dialogue to something more appropriate."

"As my lord pleases."

Belos gave an irritating, exaggeratedly thespian bow, and withdrew with an offended flourish.

I gazed out of the tall windows of the dining room to where the deer park shimmered in the heat. The deer would be panting under the trees in the little spinney in their parkland, their rough wet tongues hanging out.

The night would be hot and sultry. There had been no thunderstorms to give relief.

It seemed ironic that in all that enormous mansion of mine, the only person who would spend the night in comfort and not sweating and chafing with the heat would be the gypsy, imprisoned in the cold, damp cellars deep underneath the house.

The more I wilted in the dining room, the more interesting an interview with the gypsy, in his cool imprisonment, began to appear. Finally, I drained my glass and made my way to the back of the house.

Here, leading down behind an oak door, was a flight of steps that seemed to disappear into the earth. This was the last relic of the medieval Danby family who had owned the castle which had once stood on this spot. Their towers above ground had long since vanished, but their dungeons remained. Here they had exerted their feudal powers, imprisoning rebellious tenants and aggressive neighbours when they could catch them, and, when times were particularly hard, locking up anyone at all from whom they might expect a decent ransom. They were average feudal thugs.

The rooms at the foot of the staircase were actually caves, hollowed out of the solid rock on which the castle had been built.

The dungeons had been intended to bring about the appropriate sense of fear or repentance in the Danbys' prisoners. They were as damp and cold as could be contrived without actually extinguishing life. One of Lord Charles Danby's architects had toyed with the idea of converting them into a Gothic crypt, but the wet running down the walls had washed away his enthusiasm. My grandfather, old Hedger, saw no point in any expenditure at all on the cellars. He did not intend to extend his wine stores into them, preferring ale himself, and was unwilling to do anything more than provide a stout door to make sure the cellars were shut off.

I felt the cool air striking up from the depths at the bottom of the staircase.

At the foot of the stairs, a dim light burned in an iron mount on the wall. There was a grille fitted to the wall of the cell. I peered through its bars for a minute or two before I turned the key in the lock and entered.

The man was seated at a rough table in the middle of the room. His head was propped on his hands. His hair hung loose and disordered in thick black locks, shiny with grease in the rushlight. He was crooning something to himself:

> *"Kek man camov te jib bolli-mengreskoenaes,*
> *Man camov te jib weshenjugalogonaes."*

I recognised it as a fragment of an old Romany song:

> *"I do not wish to live like a Christian,*
> *I wish to live like a dog of the wood."*

The "dog of the wood" is the fox, in the old gypsy speech. The man was of the real old gypsy clan, who wander from India to the distant northern wastes, and whom I had encountered in my own roamings; I had endeavoured to learn a little of their talk at one time, and had even jotted down some phrases in a notebook. The man I had rescued was a *kaulo* Romany, a "black Romany" in their own tongue. They will not sleep in a house nor enter a church, and say that a curse will befall any of their children who bury their parents in a churchyard.

Was this the man who had killed the Crawshays, father and son, raising, aiming and firing first one pistol, then the next? Perhaps. This was, after all, the man whom Marie had described bending over the bodies when she had peered through the crack in the door.

There was a heavy bar across the outside of the door, and I raised it. As I entered the cell, the gypsy stood up from the table, but quietly, unthreateningly: I did not fear him. He was like an animal that has recently been caged, but has ceased to struggle.

There was some blood on the front of his dirty shirt, but that could have come from the cut on his lip: I had myself seen the blood dripping down from his face when he had been tied to the wheel of the cart in the farmhouse yard.

There was plenty of evidence against him. I rehearsed it in my mind. There was the testimony of Marie Crawshay, who had seen him standing over the bodies with her own eyes. But it was not Marie's word alone that damned him. Some of the men had seized the gypsy and searched him, and had found a bundle of linen. Wrapped in a child's shirt buried in the depths of the bundle were the guineas. And Crawshay's heavy silver fob watch, taken from his dead body.

I could hear the voice of the prosecution in court, of the lawyer holding up that very watch for the eyes of the jury: "And whence gentlemen of the jury, whence had he come by these items, the linen and the watch? Why, he said that Mistress Crawshay had given them to him! Did you ever hear such a wicked tarradiddle! He claims that she gave him some old linen, and he did not know that gold and silver lay wrapped within it! And when those stout fellows from the village detained him, and opened the bundle before his very eyes, why, who was more surprised than he, when out rolled the guineas and the watch! And he, the gypsy-man, he had never known that there was anything inside the bundle of old linen that Mistress Crawshay had furnished him with!

"I ask you, gentlemen of the jury, was there ever such a wicked tissue of lies?"

And then the prosecutor would put the final nail in the gypsy's coffin. Holding up the watch, gleaming silver in the light through the courtroom windows:

"And there, gentlemen of the jury, is the watch taken even from the body, the still-warm corpse, of Farmer Crawshay! From the dead body of one of the honest yeomen of England! And that smear upon it, gentlemen, why, that is the blood of the murdered man, upon it still!"

"Gentlemen of the jury, what is your verdict?" The judge's voice, droning, uninterested, the outcome a foregone conclusion, his clerk already holding the black cap over his lordship's frazzled old wig.

"Guilty, upon my honour!"

But there was one problem still in my mind. There was not *enough* blood in all this.

Anyone unused to the sight of sudden death from pistol wounds might have thought there was blood in plenty, but I had seen many men killed in such a way, and the effect at such close quarters was inevitably to spatter blood and brains like a fountain. Some would splash on the walls, some would collect in pools under the bodies, as I had observed on the table and floor at the farm.

And there should be some on the murderer, who had stood so close to the victims as the deadly shots were fired. Yet the only signs on any personage had been the mark on the bosom of the governess's velvet dress, and the obscure smears on the child's shirt in which the guineas and the silver watch had been wrapped. No blood on the gypsy, who had committed the murder and afterwards rifled one of the dead, except such as might well have come from his own cuts and abrasions. No blood on Marie Crawshay, who had discovered the bodies of her father-in-law and her husband. Had she not brushed against them, not leaned over them, nor in her terror and grief touched them, felt the stillness of death upon their bodies, cradled her husband in her arms? None of those things, evidently, for if she had, her dress must have borne traces of it.

I recalled a few words of the gypsy's language.

"Hokka tute mande htavava tute!"

That is to say: "If you tell me a falsehood, I will kill you!"

He moved back in astonishment, taken by surprise at hearing the words. I took the rushlight from its iron holder and held it closer to the gypsy's face. The huge dark eyes, without fire, seemed like the great mournful eyes of cattle. He pulled back a little from the light.

"It wasna' me, your lordship. I did naught there, at Crawshay's. They was good to me at Crawshay's. The *givengro* was good to me."

He used an ancient word for farmer: *givengro*, the wheatfellow, one who grows crops and settles the land, not one of us, the gypsies and we who roam free. His accent was strange, unfamiliar to me, and to the villagers he might have been speaking in the voice of the devil itself. His words rushed on.

"I was nowhere near the house, I swear to your honour, I swear it on the life of my child, when they was killed, the old man and the young master. I was walking in the fields, on the way to Crawshay's, when I heard the shots—if any man saw me then, they could prove that I was not guilty."

Hopeless chance, thought I, for if anyone in this district knew of aught that would prove the gypsy's innocence, would they come forward? Not the slightest possibility, for he was guilty, as the country folk here had decided amongst themselves, and any who gainsaid this lawless verdict would doubtless lose all popularity amongst their fellows. No, no one would come forward to testify that they had seen the Romany man walking through the fields as the shots that killed the Crawshays were fired.

But he was not finished.

"I heard the sounds, lord, but, God forgive me, I thought nothing of it. First one shot, then another, a little while later."

"A little while later, say you?"

This was strange. And, therefore, interesting to my jaded mind.

"How long afterwards? How long between the shots?"

"A while, lord."

A deeply irritating answer, but I could not show my impatience: most of these country folk have no sense of time by the clock, even in this day and age when elsewhere there is a busy world of scientific invention. Why, I read but lately in one of Belos's old newspapers (no more than three months stale, I promise you) that an inhabitant of Ayr in North Britain, one Dick Irvine, has taken out patents for an improved railroad and method of propelling carriages thereon, and a Mr. Gurney has invented a steam carriage that will run on four wheels. Yet here, men still tell the time by the sun rolling round the sky, and if it rains and the sun is obscured, why, they cannot work in the fields anyway, so there's an end on it. But as for knowing the hour by any other means, that is beyond the bumpkins hereabouts. The better houses have long-case clocks, a farmer like Crawshay carries a lumpy silver timepiece in his pocket, but for the rest, time is measured as it was for their ancestors five hundred years ago. The villagers take their time from the church bells, and a man such as this gypsy would read his hours in the passing of the sun across the heavens. I doubted he could tell the time from a clock if it were shown to him.

Still, no point in showing any impatience.

"A long while, would you say?"

This time I got a surprisingly sensible response.

"The space of time it took me to walk across Quillan's Field. I were at the bottom of the field when I heard the first shot, and near the top of the rise at t' other end when there came the second."

I knew Quillan's Field; this was an old name in the district for a patch of ground that lay between the place where the gypsy family was encamped and the Crawshay farmhouse. I calculated it would take an active man a few minutes, or a little longer, to cross it. About five minutes, perhaps?

Had not Marie Crawshay spoken of the shots as if they had been fired almost together? I tried to recall her words: "I heard a couple of loud bangs from the direction of the house." Perhaps I had just assumed the sounds were close together.

So why might there have been a delay between the shots of the pistols that had killed the men in the farmhouse? Both guns had been fired; the murderer would not have had to reload.

What had the killer been doing between the shots? There might have been a fight, of course: one of the Crawshays might have grappled with the murderer before the second shot could be fired. But there was no sign of a disturbance in that room where the killings had taken place. Nothing overturned or broken.

"What did you think when you heard the shots?"

"I thought nothing, lord."

That I could certainly credit.

"Thought they was after rabbits or pheasants in the corn stubble near the house. 'Tis nothing, a few gunshots round a farm. Course, I did not know they was from inside the farm. And when I got there, all seemed to be as it always was and Mistress Crawshay gave me a bundle of clothes—she were like goodness itself to us. I went no further in than the kitchen. I believed naught was wrong in that house, and that's the truth. I swear it, *O raia*—O lord. I hurt none at

Crawshay's! Mistress Crawshay gave me the old shirt—she gave it me!"

I broke through his protests.

"It will not be for me to try you. You can save your breath—it's no use pleading with me. You may face the *nashimescro* yet."

The *nashimescro* is the hangman, a figure with whom the gypsies, persecuted as they are throughout Europe, are only too well acquainted.

He was ever more agitated.

"My *romany chi ta chavali*. My gypsy-woman and my child—I fear for them more than for myself. She and my girl—they be still in the *keir vardo,* the caravan, near Quillan's, where any men can get them if they do so please, and they will torment them sorely. Those men are the animals, though they say Romanies are no better than the beasts. Let them have me, take me out and give me to the men at Crawshay's, but help my woman and the little *chavali*!"

"I can do nothing more for you—haven't I already said so?"

He fell back on the straw, silent and despairing. Yet, as I turned and began to mount the stairs, he called after me:

"You could save them, my lord! You could!"

I could no longer hear the man's cries. Malfine was empty, silent in the heat, as I climbed the stone steps and passed over the marble floors that echoed under my feet.

The thought of the gypsy's family edged into my mind again, though I pushed it away. I supposed they were ragged, thin and dark creatures, like the man himself, alien in their looks to the native dwellers in the English countryside. They were outsiders, with no one to speak for or protect them. The caravan sitting defenceless in a clearing, a mob gathering around it . . . I thought of the faces I had seen at the farm, filled with rage and hate.

Perhaps there was something I might do.

If I could be roused to it.

I found myself a while later unlocking a cupboard in my

bedroom, and taking out a pistol. A plain and unadorned workaday weapon. Nothing flashy, no engraved barrel or chased mounts, quite unlike the duellist's weapons at the farmhouse. Only a gunsmith would have recognised its quality—a piece of blue metal with the deep watered-silk gleam of tempered steel.

But why should I do aught? I had saved the man himself, saved him for his trial, and that was both the full extent of my obligation and beyond my inclination. The whole affair was nothing more to do with me.

CHAPTER 7

THE afternoon still held much of its heat as I rode Zaraband along a bridle path skirting the crops. Dust rose up from her hooves as we passed between the fields, some with the stubble of harvest, others still with their burden of ripened wheat waiting for the harvester's scythe. The heat haze shimmered and the mare's hooves made little sound on the soft dust. Now and then she flicked her ears to drive away a fly, and the sun still beat down on us, though it was lower in the sky. I felt a sweat breaking out under my shirt.

The countryside seemed empty except for man and horse.

The path which I somehow found myself taking, towards Quillan's Field, led round the side of a steep little hill, farmed only on its lower slopes. I let the mare take her time going uphill, and we were moving slowly upwards along the path when there came a strange muffled thumping sound from the other side of the little knoll. Zaraband checked suddenly and whinnied nervously. There came what sounded like a human gasp, cut off as suddenly as it had begun.

I urged the mare round the slope and the group on the other side of the hill came into sight.

They looked to be country labourers; I thought at least two of them were from the village. And two were scarcely more than boys, their round, fresh faces too young and innocent to be doing what they were doing.

The woman was lying in the middle of the ring of men. One man held her arms above her head. A red garment of some sort, a scarf or a torn petticoat, perhaps, had been thrust into her mouth, cutting off her cries. Two men, kneeling as if in a gross parody of religious ecstasy, held her legs apart. Another, one hand on his belt, was pulling down his britches as he stood over her, his hairy white buttocks thrusting out as he bent forward.

I saw a small child, its face stained with dirt and tears, leap at the man who was standing over the woman. The man knocked the child back with his free hand, a vicious blow that landed with a crack on the child's face.

The woman's body was nearly naked, with her rags pulled up above her thighs. One of the kneeling men reached out and pulled the cloth from her breasts. His fingers dug into the soft flesh and the woman threshed helplessly beneath his hand.

A twig snapped under Zaraband's hooves and the group turned in my direction, and then froze like a picture.

The two boys moved back, but the men refused to give ground. They were aroused now. The man bending over the woman straightened up but made no effort to disguise his lust, nor even to pull his britches up over his thrusting flesh. His face was red, sweating, angry.

"It's the gypsy's whore. We're giving her what she deserves, that's all," he said, defiantly.

I dismounted and moved towards them. The men must have read something in my face, for although no word was spoken, one of them broke away and ran stumbling down the hill.

But the man whose pleasure had been interrupted moved threateningly towards me. A dog will fight for its lusts.

"Want her yourself, my lord? Like them dirty, do you? Take a good look at this then."

He jerked his hairy naked groin obscenely, openly. "You can have her after I've been through her."

I advanced towards him and he released his victim and hurled himself at me, his fists flying blindly.

Then he stopped short, looking down at the dark steel barrel held before his chest.

I smiled, thrust my face into his, and spoke with slow, careful contempt.

"One more step and I'll put a bullet through you."

The man had one last try at pleading.

"She's trash, my lord. Why can't us have her? She's not too dirty for the likes of us."

"I'll see you all dead first. And you know it, don't you? You know my reputation in these parts. I got these scars upon my face from killing better men than you."

The others began to back away down the hill.

The man hesitated. He began to pull his clothing over himself.

Suddenly, they broke. They turned and ran, stumbling into the wheat in their fear.

The woman was sitting up and trying to cover herself. The child, a girl I now realised, rushed fiercely in front of her mother, little teeth snarling like a young animal.

The woman said something to the child, who stood still, but the tension did not leave the small body, and she stared defiantly up at me as I spoke, carefully, simply, as one might to a frightened animal, trying to reassure it with the sound of the voice rather than the words.

"I won't hurt you. There's nothing to be frightened of now. They've all gone."

The woman answered me in English, thickly accented.

"They'll be back. They'll never leave us alone now. I might as well cut my throat and the child's too, and have done with it. They would have had the child as well, if you hadn't come along. We're just sport to them. Vermin, they call us. *Mi Dovvel opral, dik tuley opre mande!* My God above, look down on me!"

The gypsy's woman was handsome enough under the dirt and rags. Her eyes were dark and long-lashed, set in thin, slanting cheekbones. There was a dreadful air of resignation about her, a weary quietness, like an ill-treated animal, for whom one beating is scarcely over when the next begins.

She bowed her head and I had trouble following her words as she continued.

"They smashed up the caravan and set fire to it. They'd have burned us alive if we'd been inside it. We've no home, no man, *kek keir vardo, kek guero.* They'll get us the next time."

"Have you no one you could go to? Is there nowhere you could find protection?"

"We've blood kin camped near Callerton, for they've come to sell their ponies at the Callerton fair. The Lees— they'd take us in. But we'll never get to them. Them men— they'll come for us again as soon as you've gone."

I did not doubt her. They would be back, hunting these terrified hares through the darkening countryside.

"I'll get you to Callerton. We'll go to the caravan first."

The child led the way, back along a track towards the farm. Near Quillan's Field, about half a mile from the little hill where I had found the woman and her *chavali,* as the man had called the child, there was a clump of trees, and just beyond the trees we came to the caravan. Charred splinters of brightly painted wood lay all around the clearing. The caravan was smashed to pieces: it looked as if the attackers had taken an axe to it. The contents, mostly unrecognisable, were strewn all around, ripped and smashed.

The woman sat on her haunches as she surveyed the debris of her home and moaned softly, rocking to and fro. *"Bengako tan!"* she murmured. *"Bengako tan!"*

A hellish place.

For some, hell was on a distant Grecian shore. For others, it was here: in the middle of the pleasant English country-side.

The child spoke, standing in the wreckage.

"We tried to run away when they come, mister. We run in the field yonder and lay in the wheat. But they found us. They done chased us out."

I could visualise it—a gang of men from the village bursting into the clearing and setting about them, the woman and her child bolting into the wheat, their pursuers tracking them without difficulty through the trail trampled in the crops. They had been driven out on to the grassy slopes of the little hill, brown and scorched by the long summer, like small animals running from the harvesters. And then there was nowhere else to run.

The woman was calmer now. She looked up at me.

"There's none hereabouts but hates us now. Most of them would do any filthy thing they can think of. We are *mullo mas*."

Mullo mas. Dead flesh. Carrion.

It was true, I knew it from the desolation in front of me. This had been a deliberate, determined attack. News of the murder had spread through the whole district and the countryside would now be roused against all gypsies. The man suspected of the murders could not be touched—I had him safely locked up in the cellars of Malfine, had snatched him from the mob at Crawshay's. But his woman and his child were unprotected and would be easy prey.

Undoubtedly, the best course would be to take them to Callerton, where I knew the gypsies were encamped in sufficiently large numbers to deal with any attacks the locals might mount against them. If I left the woman and her child here, they would not last long.

"Find something to cover your mother," I said to the girl, for the woman was still clutching torn rags round herself. "And then see if there's anything left here worth the taking. I'll get you to Callerton."

I looked round the clearing. There might be a few pathetic possessions that could be salvaged.

Unexpectedly, the bony old horse that had pulled the caravan loomed up, quietly cropping grass beyond the trees. His frayed tethering rope trailed behind him—he must have managed to bolt from the attackers, breaking the old rope in the process. He seemed unexcited by his freedom, and stood obediently still when the child ran over and caught his halter.

The girl found an old skirt and a piece of linen with which the woman managed to cover herself. She rose and began to help the child pick over the rubbish, holding up a shard of china here, a torn blanket there. Eventually they tied up some old coverlets and a tin pan and a kettle. Nothing else seemed to have been left unscathed.

I was surprised when I saw them piling all the rubbish into a heap on the broken shell of the caravan. The woman saw the expression on my face.

"The Lees'll come back with me," she said. "They'll come back and we'll burn the rest. All this. On the day they hang him. He did not kill them, lord. My man did not kill them at Crawshay's farm. But they must have someone to hang for it. They'll hang him."

I was silent. Without another word, the woman loaded the old horse with their bundle. I lifted the child up before me on Zaraband, and the woman climbed up on the horse, and the little procession set slowly off.

The way was at first uneventful, but we had to pass through the village, and I felt the thin body of the child stiffen with fear as we approached.

A small boy came running out of one of the cottages, staring at us with round eyes, then bolted back inside, shouting for his mother.

"Mam, Mam, it's the gypsy-woman. Where's he taking her?"

A woman appeared at the door of the cottage. She stared

at us malevolently. "Leave them to us, my lord," she called up to me, made bold by hatred. She bent down, and the next thing I knew was a clod of earth flying through the air. It struck the gypsy-woman full on the chest. She did not flinch, but held her head high and stared straight ahead. The child, too, looked up defiantly, though I could feel the terror which gripped her small body.

"Don't be afraid!" I whispered. "Look straight ahead."

By twos and threes the villagers were coming out of their doors until there was an ugly little crowd. They recognised me, but their mood was threatening enough to challenge my authority as Zaraband picked her way through. A voice called out, "My lord, we'll have her!" and another answered, "We'll hang them now!" The crowd closed up in front of us, barring the muddy track that passed as the main street of the village. I hoped it would not be necessary to draw my pistol. I urged Zaraband forward and she stepped out, gently pushing her way through. The people looked angry and sullen, but still they dared not offer me violence. One of the bolder spirits laid his hands on the mare's bridle, but he stepped back as he looked up into my scarred face. Strange, how my healed wounds can serve me now: the scars of them terrify these peasants.

I saw one of the men at the back lowering a pitchfork to the ground. The angry buzz of voices fell silent and the crowd parted to let us through. We passed down the dusty track between the cottages in silence. I heard one last voice, a woman's, as we passed:

"The devil's looking after his own!"

It took about two hours to reach Callerton. We travelled slowly, holding Zaraband in check so that the gypsy's old horse could keep up.

As we drew near the town, the woman indicated a track that led off the road towards some woods. "That's where they be camped, my lord."

We turned off the road and made for the woods. The sun was going down, but the day still held some heat. The child was asleep now; her hair was none of the cleanest and a cloud of insects danced around her head as we rode along in the orange light of the setting sun, which was now outlined against the blackness of the trees.

The man who appeared in front of the mare seemed to have sprung out of the ground. He had a scarf wrapped round the lower part of his face and a wickedly curved knife gleamed at his belt. Suddenly, I realised we were surrounded by half a dozen men, moving as silently as cats. The man in front of me leaped up at the mare and pulled her to a halt. I reached for my pistol, but before I could draw it, the man fell back as the gypsy-woman shouted something. She slid down from the horse and began to talk urgently, in their Romany tongue, occasionally gesturing towards me. The man in front of the mare reached out his arms for the child, who had started awake, and now fell sleepily down into his care. The light was dying fast now.

The woman broke off their talk and came towards me.

"*Raia,* lord, these are my kin. *Paracrow tute,* I thank you, and for my child also."

The mare was receiving admiring if not downright covetous looks from some of the men, and I heard the word "*gry, gry,*" "the horse, the horse," repeated over and again. They might be friendly for the moment, but that did not stop me from feeling that the greater the distance I put between us, the safer I should be.

I started to turn Zaraband's head towards the road, and was moving away when there was a commotion behind me and the gypsy-woman came running after.

"Lord, we owe you a gift."

I had to bend over her to hear what she was saying, for her accent made it difficult to understand, though her words were almost formal, as if in some tradition of her own.

"There is something I will tell you," she was saying. "That is my gift.

"The woman at the farm. Be wary of her, lord. And tell your servant to be wary of her also."

She reached up and grasped my sleeve, and looked up into my eyes.

"*Raia,* you are a searcher, a *jinney mengro,* that I can see. I will help you in your search. I will help the hawk in his hunting, but you must listen carefully. Listen."

I bent down and she muttered something. She had to repeat it several times before I understood that it was the name of a place.

Then she added a few more words, so that I knew why it was something important that she had told me. Something of value: knowledge, a real gift, in return for the protection I had given.

By now, it was dark, and I turned for home.

CHAPTER 8

IT was an oppressive, sticky night, yet not completely dark: it was still the light-grey night of northern summers. I woke near dawn and could not return to sleep, thinking over what the gypsies had told me, the man and the woman both. Finally, I arose from my bed, sluiced myself with cool water, took a pull of brandy, and still sleep evaded me, and all because I was engaged by this absurd rustic puzzle that chance had put in my way. A thousand times I tried to put it out of my mind. Why should I take any responsibility for the affairs of these country folk? Yet it was an intriguing problem. If the gypsy was innocent of the killings at Crawshay's, who was guilty?

I pulled on a shirt and breeches, descended from my bedroom, crossed the silent hall and stepped out from the portico of Malfine into the thinning night; if I could not sleep I might as well get up and exercise my limbs, pace through the woods to aid my thoughts.

What if the gypsy had not committed the murders? Who were possible candidates for the role of murderer? Or murderess. There were the two women, Marie Crawshay and Elisabeth Anstruther.

At this point, old Sir Anderton would have cried out in horror. "Suspect a woman! Believe a simple farmer's wife or a ladylike governess capable of murder! The idea is monstrous!"

Not monstrous to one who has seen something of the world, nor impossible to a mistrustful cynic whose faith in his fellow man—and woman—has long been shattered. Let us look firmly, fairly and squarely at the possibilities, I said to myself.

I thought about the weapons, those old pistols, and pictured them in the hands of their original owner, some elegant marksman, perhaps, who stood in the mists of some early morning, aiming at his opponent . . . They were duelling pistols, of course . . .

A duel: was it possible . . .? Had the old man and his son engaged in some bizarre contest and shot each other in a duel of some rustic sort?

But they had not been facing directly opposite each other when they died, and furthermore, even if it were to be supposed that the Crawshays, father and son, had somehow quarrelled so bitterly that they were prepared to kill each other, from what I knew of the character of the old man, he would have laughed at any such gentlemanly notion as duelling. More likely, he would have felled his son with his fist, or else he might have brandished some bucolic implement that lay ready to hand, a scrattern or a dibbler or some such I-know-not-what.

I was striding past the lake now; early-morning mists were rising from its surface. An irrelevant thought intruded: there was something missing from my excursions in the grounds of Malfine. I must get a dog to accompany me on my walks, a greyhound perhaps, who could also keep up at Zaraband's heels, a silent shadow to flit behind us through the woods. My last hound, my famously faithful Silver-jacket, died in Greece.

The Crawshay murders were a distraction from my memories.

Marie Crawshay could have committed the killings, physically. It would have taken no bodily strength to do so, though the murderer would have needed nerves of steel to kill the two men at virtually point-blank range. Crawshay had been shot full in the front of the throat, so his killer must have been looking straight at him. I tried to imagine the frail and delicate woman I had seen in the farmhouse parlour facing up to the explosive and bullying old man, firing a pistol directly at him and then turning and shooting her own husband in the face, through the jaw. Did Marie have the will and strength of mind to carry all that out? She seemed feverish with laudanum: if she were a habitual user of the drug, unstable and excitable as it usually rendered its addicts, she would surely not have the determination to execute the murders. And she would have to be a most plausible liar, to tell me that circumstantially detailed tale of how she had stood in the barn and heard the shots that killed the Crawshays.

But weighing most deeply against the possibility that Marie was a murderess was the apparent absence of any motivation for a *double* killing. The old man—yes, perhaps if there had been quarrels, if she hoped Edmund would inherit the farm, yes she might have killed old Crawshay. But why, in that case, would she have murdered her own husband, the pliable-sounding Edmund, who would be the heir to everything?

And if Marie had some motive for killing one or the other of the men, she would have had plenty of other chances. It was absurd that she should fire on the men when they were together, when she had ample opportunities for finding her victim alone. Together, the Crawshays presented a formidable problem to an attacker, for whichever was first struck down, the other would turn on the murderer, and presumably even Edmund was capable of fighting for his life. Of course, they could have been killed with simultaneous shots, but they had been seated at different sides of the table when death had struck them, so that it would have been an extraordinarily difficult feat of marksmanship to bring them down together, killing both instantaneously. To kill them both in the same moment, the murderer would have had to have a pistol in either hand, and aim and fire both weapons in virtually one second. A farmer's wife would know how to fire a gun, but she was unlikely to be a skilled and deadly shot.

The same surely applied to the governess. I walked on through the woods, pondering this possibility, and now I could see the houses of the village looming up like haystacks in the distance.

Again, it was possible that Elisabeth Anstruther could have committed the crimes. I had known little of her before my visit to Crawshay's, and had learned little since. Certainly, I would judge that she had the nerve to carry out the murders, for she had seemed composed and controlled enough. But again, there was the problem of a cause: why should she kill the Crawshays when they were her employers and benefactors?

But let me suppose that for some reason Elisabeth Anstruther wanted to kill the Crawshays, father and son: if the governess was guilty, then Marie Crawshay was innocent, and she had no reason to lie in giving her account of events. And she, trembling in the barn with her little son, had apparently heard the shots *before* Elisabeth Anstruther had arrived in the pony-cart.

Who else might there be? Some discontented worker, some labourer turned off Crawshay land, perhaps? Someone who had been prepared to take the risk of being seen by Marie or the governess? Or perhaps someone more accustomed to firearms—someone like Sir Anderton himself, a good shot and without a nerve in his body? Anderton could well have had some quarrel with the Crawshays, over some such local dispute as land boundaries, perhaps, and stridden out to the farm in a high old rage. He was choleric enough to take a pot-shot at anyone who gainsaid him, though I did not think that cold-blooded murder was his style.

In any case, I remembered, old Anderton was in London.

I was nearly at the outskirts of the little huddle of houses by now. Our village is made of the most primitive elements, out of the very ground it springs from, so it seems. The biggest structure it boasts is the alehouse, which is larger than the tumbledown little church, a miserable Gothic heap. We have no parson—a curate comes over from Callerton on a Sunday to give a service and harangue the rustics.

The houses—if I can dignify them with such an appellation—the houses which ramble along the single village street—a track, merely—are built of mud itself. They are made of unfired clay, or cob, as they say in these parts, manufactured in the most simple fashion. I used to watch it being done, when I was a boy. The mud is trampled down, with some straw admixed, into a semblance of some solidity, and then lumps of this trodden earth are rammed on top of one another to form the walls. A thatched roof, more or less ragged, is raised upon the cob walls: one room downstairs and one aloft suffice for the entire household. Very pretty they can look in summer, those hovels that are whitewashed with a little lime and neatly roofed, but they are best admired from afar, I promise you. There are gentlefolk who praise the Picturesque in cottages—and those who sketch them, but always at a distance, I have noted, and sitting upwind of the middens.

"Cool in summer and warm in winter" is said of cob houses—to which might be added "and damp all year round"; those who proclaim the charm of these dwellings seldom live in them, and when they do, can afford plenty of fuel to drive the wet out of the walls, and plenty of thatch on top to keep off the rain. For those who cannot afford such luxuries, the mud houses can dissolve over their very heads—why, there was an old woman who was washed out of her house while still lying in her bed, once when a heavy rainstorm flooded the village. For such houses as survive inclemencies, the weathering gives the local architecture, if we can dignify it with that name, a pleasing, gently rounded appearance; pleasing, that is, if you yourself live safely within walls of brick or stone.

Still, in the half-light of early morning, the dim outlines of the village looked attractive enough, the weathered thatches hunkering down upon the low walls, and dawn was just breaking.

Our eyes deceive us in such a light, and I was at first mistrustful of a form that seemed to be fashioned out of the mist itself: I narrowed my eyes and peered through the greyish light. Yes, that dim outline that I could espy in the distance was indeed a human shape, slipping along behind the hedges, following the dusty track of the coach road that led to the village. The movements were slinking and furtive, for the fellow did not walk along the road like an honest man, but crept about along the scrubby bushes. He was taking care not to be seen from the road, but did not perceive that I, walking along the path that led from Malfine woods to the village, could see him outlined on the horizon against the growing light of day.

Somewhere, in one of the houses, a dog barked, and yelped as it was cuffed. The form crouched down behind the hedgerow.

I stopped in my tracks, stood silently, watching.

The creature behind the hedge waited for a few moments, and then, when the barking of the dog appeared not to have aroused any alarm, moved onwards. The light was better now, and I could see more clearly. The man was limping, dragging one foot painfully behind, yet moving steadily, determinedly. Moving fast. At this distance, I could not make out any of the details of his appearance.

Now the flickering light of a candle appeared in the still-dark window of a cottage at the outskirts of the village, and I could see a figure appear within the room, passing and repassing the casement, and I heard the crying of a child. It was a woman, nursing a fretful baby.

The shape crept closer to this cottage, slowly and carefully, crouching down, and then peered in the window. He seemed to stare as if hypnotised for a few moments; then he slipped past the windowsill to the door and laid his hand upon the latch. There was a long, easy, malevolent deliberation in his actions.

So there was an outsider skulking about the village—a candidate for the role of murderer. An outsider—that would let everyone off the hook: the women at Crawshay's would be clear of all suspicion, there would be no need for finger-pointing and mistrust among the villagers, and the gypsy, whom Lord Ambrose had quixotically taken it into his scarred and aristocratic head to rescue, could be released.

I quickened my pace towards the distant form, but then, just as I was hastening towards the cottage, he stopped and pulled himself away from the door, and limped off as fast as his crippled limb would allow, as if he were bent on a different track and would not be turned aside for anything else, like an animal that has scented a particular quarry and will hunt it down to the end, ignoring lesser game.

He would not be sidetracked.

Those were the thoughts that came into my mind as I saw the crippled man slip away, a darker shadow against the bright dawn.

CHAPTER 9

BACK at Malfine, although it was so early in the day, there was a welcome clatter from the kitchen and smells of bacon and mushrooms were drifting up to the library, where I took breakfast on my return. My appetite, which had been but feeble and unappreciative during the long months of convalescence, seemed to be returning. Belos laid a silver-covered dish in front of me, and I swept off the lid and helped myself to the glistening rashers. Belos was pouring coffee from a silver pot. He insisted on these refinements: I would as soon have breakfasted as I recollected doing in my youth, running into the kitchen, hacking a thick slice of bacon from a joint that hung in the larder, laying it in a heavy copper frying pan, and downing a quart of champagne as I waited impatiently for my rough-and-ready meal to sizzle and crisp, but Belos would never have allowed this unseemly behaviour.

"Belos, have you ever seen a crippled man skulking around the village? Or ever heard talk of one?"

"I don't recall any such, my lord. Of course, there is old Tyler, Sir Anderton's former gamekeeper, but he is a complete invalid, I understand, and cannot so much as leave his bed."

"No, the man I saw this morning—at least, I'm almost certain I saw him, but the light was bad, I grant you—he was lame, but he could move pretty fast, like a young man. D'you think he's a stranger here?"

"I think he must be, my lord."

"Then there's cause for concern, Belos, if we have someone creeping about in these parts."

What really flashed through my mind, of course, was that the stranger might be implicated in the murders at Crawshay's farm.

"You are doubtless thinking that this has something to do with the murders, my lord?"

"Damn you, Belos, you're too quick. This bacon is superb. Afterwards, I think I'll go over to the farm."

"You are active this morning, my lord. Shall I have Zaraband saddled and brought round?"

"Yes, but give me some more of those mushrooms first."

" 'Now good digestion wait on appetite, And health on both!' "

"Where does that come from? I don't recognise it."

"The Scottish play again, my lord. The banquet scene. I once played Banquo—and his ghost, of course—at the Theatre Royal in Bristol."

"Hardly a good omen, Belos!"

But I tucked in cheerfully enough.

Afterwards, there was something which made me feel uneasy: the bodies of the Crawshays. They should be in the icehouse by now, but I wanted to check, and to examine them again, to see if there was anything I had missed at the farmhouse. Saving the gypsy had seemed the most important action at the time, but now perhaps was the moment to consider the dead men more carefully. The icehouse was on the way to Crawshay's farm, if I followed the tracks that led across country.

The wood lay beyond the smooth expanse of lawn which was kept short by the herd of ornamental deer. These were the descendants of a herd which my father had imported for the delight of my mother; the deer were too small and thin-legged to provide decent haunches of venison. My grandfather, greedy old man, had been much against the purchase of these useless creatures, but in the end had ceased his objections, when he had been persuaded to see them as animated hairy lawn-clippers rather than as mere adornments.

At the end of the lawn, a ditch, in which a stream usually ran, kept them from straying too far. There was a little rustic bridge with a willow gateway which prevented them from crossing the water, which had dried up in the heat of this summer.

Zaraband took the dry stream bed in an easy leap and entered the wood. A sweet pine smell reached me. The trees breathed out their scents, even in the cool morning air. There was no sound except the soft thudding of the horse's hooves, and the occasional crack in the undergrowth, the small flutters and rustlings of creatures frightened from their nests and shelters in the spider's-web dews of dawn.

The icehouse was in the centre of the wood, but I did not want to take Zaraband close up to it; I remembered her nervous reaction when we had neared Crawshay's yesterday, and she had scented the foul air with those delicate nostrils. She was not an old battle-horse, hardened to smells of death and decay, and I tethered her to a tree just inside the fringes of the wood.

I had prepared myself, as I neared the icehouse, and pulled from my pocket a linen handkerchief soaked in cologne. I did not care much for the sickly odour of the scent, but at least it masked some of the evidence of mortality that grew more powerful as I neared the icehouse, contaminating the clean morning air.

The icehouse was a mock-Gothic folly. It was topped by all sorts of curious little pinnacles, so that it resembled a tiny castle. There were only narrow slits for windows, very high up and shaded with shingles so as to exclude the sun as much as possible. It had been the fantasy of the architect to make these absurd and useless windows into arrow slits, like those in the towers of Gothic castles.

A huge and thick door, quite suitable for a medieval castle, had been crafted to fit tightly so that no chink of light, which would speed the melting of the ice, would be admitted through the entrance. There was a lock in the door, deemed necessary because ice was, after all, a precious substance, preserved with difficulty and not to be enjoyed by the vulgar, except in winter, when they might have as much as they pleased.

The padlock, which would normally have been rusty, gleamed, hanging on the door jamb. This did not alert me, for it was my thought that Tom, when he arranged for the corpses of the Crawshays to be deposited here, had cleaned and oiled the lock. The key was somewhere on a board in the gun room at Malfine, where it was kept with a load of other such rusty old implements, some with crabbed script on yellowing labels: "Housekeeper's Closets"; "Pleaching Shed"; "Boot Room"; "Icehouse." Belos would doubtless have identified the right key and brought it over to the men at the farm.

The door was not locked.

I pushed it inward on its hinges and descended the short flight of steps inside. The building, to a depth of about ten feet, was entirely below ground.

The floor was marble, and it struck cold to my feet.

There was more marble, placed in slabs like low tables, with drains and channels to carry the water away as the great blocks of ice on the slabs slowly dripped away in here.

Instead of the ice, the bodies of Crawshay and his son lay on the slabs, placed there according to my instructions. There was some oozing from the corpses, their fluids draining along the marble channels cut for the melting ice, as if the bodies lay on a purpose-built table for chirurgical dissection.

I stepped into the middle of the floor, my boots treading in a slippery liquid, and looked again at the dead men

I had seen in the outhouse at Crawshay's farm. I did not wish to linger, but I had to do my duty: when the coroner's jury met, it would have to examine these bodies, and I had to make sure they would be available for the jurymen's grisly attentions. Stories of the horrors they had witnessed—of the black faces, the bellies swollen with gases—would be retailed in the district with the greatest relish by those same jurors, whose protests of reluctance to perform their traditional task of viewing the bodies of the victims were mitigated by their anxiety to be the centre of attention when the tale was relayed to other turnips, agog for details.

The bodies were intact and ready for the jurors' inspection, or at least, they were decaying only by natural processes. Sadly for scaremongers, no local witches or werewolves had intervened in picturesque rustic fashion, no hands had been severed to soak in wax and turn into candles, it seemed that no ghoulish souvenir-hunters had clipped off bits of clothing or locks of hair. The two men lay, stretched out on their slabs, as decently as bloody and rotting corpses may.

My bravado ceased.

Old Crawshay's face seemed to move in the gloom.

Closer, closer, and in the dim light from the door I could see that the maggots were already squirming in his eyes.

Yet there was something I must look at. Something I had not noticed in the farm outhouse, but was now visible in the light from the partly opened door.

Strands of long hair entwined round the horn buttons of the old man's waistcoat. Long, streaming hair, dabbled with the blood from the wound in his neck.

Bending over the body, repressing my nausea, I pulled four or five of the hairs from the buttons and thrust them into my breeches pocket.

I turned and made for the door, even my hardened stomach beginning to turn, but as I climbed the steps that led out of the icehouse, the door seemed for a moment to fly wide open, and I was blinded by a ray of brilliant sun that shone out into the darkness like a sword.

Something struck me full in the breast, and I fell back down the steps, slipped on the wet marble floor at the bottom, and heard the door above me slam shut with a crash.

Only the faintest chinks of light reached me through the door of the icehouse. I stumbled in the gloom.

After a few minutes, my eyes became accustomed to it and I could dimly make out the shapes of the dead men lying on their marble slabs. I did not care for the thought of slithering about on that slippery floor, and perhaps falling on to their flesh, grown soft and jelly-like with the onset of decay.

My thoughts were like reluctant horses trying to bolt from a fence. I tried to think rationally about what might be happening in that brightly lit morning outside the icehouse.

Could the door have slammed shut by chance? I groped my way to the top of the steps and pushed against it, but it did not give an inch. The door must have been shut by a human agency, then, for someone had also turned the key in the lock. I called and shouted.

A waste of breath.

The roof of the icehouse seemed to ring with my cries, but no one came.

There was no point in exhausting myself with shouting. I had to consider my position.

There was no chance of battering down the door. It was my ill-fortune that the carpenter had been an honest man. Good hard seasoned wood had been carefully fitted into the frame of the door. Even if I could find something—a piece of marble, say—that could be used as a battering-ram, I would be unable to get up any momentum, because I would have to charge up that flight of steps inside the door.

There remained for consideration the windows, high above me, admitting mere slits of light. They were about two feet long and about the width of the palm of the hand. Would it be possible to clamber up and trail something out of them—a piece of my shirt, perhaps, something that would alert any passer-by?

Passer-by? Tush, I said to myself, do you think you are in Piccadilly? There will be no passers-by here, no strollers enjoying the air and the fashions. You are buried in the depths of the countryside and surrounded by wilderness; no bumpkins will come idling round here, you may be sure.

I tried dragging some spare slabs of marble across the floor to form a kind of staircase which stretched treacherously upwards towards the windows, and succeeded only in ripping my hands on jagged edges of marble, and bruising a shin when I fell back to the floor.

Time to think more rationally.

If I had been shut in here accidentally, there was no likelihood that the person responsible would return. Why should they? If they had simply seen the door open, thought that it should have been closed, and slammed it, then they might have no idea that they had condemned a man to imprisonment with the dead. It might have been some well-intentioned turnip, who knew that the bodies had been placed in the icehouse, thought that the door should be secured, and was even now glowing with satisfaction at having performed a small social duty. Why should such a person, entirely ignorant of the consequences of their actions, bother to return?

There was in fact no legitimate reason for anyone to come to the icehouse, not until Jeffries, the coroner, fixed a day for the inquest, and that might be several weeks away. Perhaps not that long: even that old fool must realise what would happen to the cadavers in this heat. But long enough, for one locked in, as I was, with nothing but the bodies of the murdered men.

Zaraband would be found, of course, eventually, tethered at some distance, so that there was nothing to connect my disappearance with the icehouse. Indeed, I had not mentioned it to Belos: I had merely told him I was going to Crawshay's farm. They would look for me there, if anywhere. There might have been a chance of stray lovers coming to the ice-house, or poachers who wanted to use it as a temporary larder for their bag of pheasant or rabbit. But my hopes of such innocents accidentally stumbling on my imprisonment soon faded. News would have spread rapidly that the bodies of the Crawshays had been placed here. No one would come to make love in front of those silent pieces of flesh, no poachers would hang up their venison over a pair of corpses.

There was only one chance of release, and I did not care to face it.

If I had been imprisoned intentionally, my persecutor might come back to gloat.

If someone had a mind sufficiently perverted to play this trick on me, that person would want to come back and see the victim, myself, gibbering with fright.

Well, I refused to gibber. I had seen too many dead men to fear these two dull English farmers, boring and prosaic even on their marble slabs.

In the meantime, how long could I last?

I began to think carefully about it. I could live without food for a week or more. This I knew, for I had done so in Greece. Once I was with a band of irregulars—bandits to the Turks, heroes to the Greeks—and the whole brigade had taken refuge from pursuit in a hidden cave, where we laid up for six days.

There was a Turkish camp which had been set up in the valley under the mouth of the cave, concealed in a grey cleft of the mountainous rocks above. After those six days, the Turkish soldiers struck their tents and moved away, puzzled, because a prey which had seemed just before them had apparently vanished into the mountains. We had kept total silence in that cave, had pulled our scarlet cummerbunds tight around our empty bellies. We dispatched our wounded comrades with our sabres, lest their cries of pain betray us. It was the first time I had killed in cold blood, and I remember the wet feel of the dying man's mouth under the palm of my hand, pressed against his lips to gag him as I drew the cutting edge across his throat.

But we had water in that cave: a pure mountain spring that gushed out in a little stream at the back of the cave, a life-saving trickle down the quartzy rock.

I must have water. Without it, I could not, in this heat, hold out for more than a day or two. Even down here it would get very hot in the middle of the day. I might manage to get up some of that slithery moisture from the floor, soaking it up in my shirt. But if that liquid were contaminated by the fluids from the bodies themselves, then I were better to be raging with thirst than to touch a drop of it. If there were some water condensing on the walls, then perhaps that would be safe.

I sat on the steps near the door and let my head sink into my hands, listening to every little sound from the outside world. Birds were singing in the trees, which rustled occasionally in a faint breeze, but no human sounds followed the rustling. Nature alone was at work outside.

Tormentingly now, I fancied that I could hear the rushing of a stream which I remembered from my boyhood, a pure, cold stream in the woods near this very spot, a stream that had never run dry in those endless summers when I was a child. There I had fished, with rods made out of hazel wands and string, with a wriggling worm stuck on a makeshift hook. I felt again the icy chill against my calves as I waded into the centre of the rushing water.

It seemed unlikely, at the moment, that I would see that stream again. I sank into a reverie, recalling that distant boyhood, and must have slept for a while, dreaming of the past. I thought of my sister, Ariadne, who had refused to return home to Malfine. Why should she? The house held no childhood memories for her, and she had chosen to make her life elsewhere.

After Ariadne's birth my mother did not seem to get stronger. In fact, she seemed fainter day by day. I, by then some nine or ten years of age, was left to play in a corner of her bedroom, listening to the whisperings and the muttered consultations, holding the pomegranate jewel up to the rays of light from the watery panes of glass in the windows. Old Eufemia, the stout maid, muttered about blood flows that could not be staunched, about swellings and clots that came away, and my mother got paler and weaker till she lay in bed all day, with a thin and terrible odour, that I now know is the smell of death from an inner disease, arising from her bed under the aura of perfume, the patchouli and attar of roses with which her linen was splashed.

For a year after her death, my father shut himself up in the suite of rooms that my mother had occupied. All pretence that he was nothing but a phlegmatic English squire, ruddy-cheeked and impervious to suffering, now vanished. The young man who had fallen so desperately in love with a beautiful Greek girl suddenly reappeared, stricken to the heart by the loss of her. He slept and ate in semi-darkness, never leaving her rooms. The curtains were always closed; he slept in the bed where she had died.

He did not speak a word to his children. We were looked after by old Eufemia, one of my mother's maids, for a while, but then the Greek servants were sent back to Italy, for they reminded my father too much of my mother. Ariadne and I were abandoned to a succession of nursemaids, until I went off to school, and Ariadne was taken away by one of my father's female cousins. In the meantime, I ran wild, eating hand to mouth when I could in the kitchen, running about in the woods as I pleased, grieving, frightened and exhilarated by turns.

When my father finally emerged from his seclusion, he had lost weight and aged greatly. The cousin who came later on to speak to him about Ariadne's care and education did not recognise him.

As for my father, he appeared to recognise no one, except for his little daughter. When she was brought to him, in the hope that she would prove to be a consolation, he began to rave and curse at her as the cause of her mother's death, which he seemed to blame entirely on the child. He begged his cousin to take the little thing away, and never let him look on her face again. He made ample payment for her to be reared and schooled as became her rank, but he would not have the child at Malfine, and attempts to reason with him provoked such a fearful rage that the cousin, who fortunately grew genuinely fond of the little girl, did not dare try the experiment of leaving the child with her father.

And it was now that the name of Danby was expunged from the district, for the machinery of bribes and loans, of sweeteners and softeners, which my grandfather, old Hedger, had started, came to fruition at last and my father, George, was offered a title in token of his father's discreet financial services to royalty. So mad was he still about his wife's death that he renamed the Danby lands after Mala Fina, the estate which her family had once owned in Crete, and asked permission to take his own title from that, so that the name of her ancestors would never die and so that I, as her son, would have an inheritance from my mother, even if it were only a claim to some remote and rocky shores in the Aegean. Mala Fina became, Englished, Malfine.

Thus Castle Danby was no more, and the mansion now bore the name of Malfine, my mother's memorial in England, though in the depths of the English countryside the name was mangled horribly, being both foreign and newfangled. And I staked my claim also, with the idiot idealism of youth, not only to Malfine but to my Cretan inheritance, a forgotten Venetian castle beside the wine-dark sea of Greece, for which I later fought, and almost died.

My mother, Eurydice, had made few changes in her husband's home. She had put up hangings of rich Italian silks and velvets. George ordered these to be taken down and folded away. They were placed in carved cedarwood chests in her room: the striped satins and the flock-piled velvets in dark colours, crimson and madonna blue and a velvety grape colour that I remember stroking with my child's fingers as if it were a live pelt, they were folded away from the light and shut up with bags of lavender and tiny grey pieces of ambergris that gave out last waves of rich scent as the lids of the wooden chests were closed tight upon them.

Shut away too were my mother's clothes: the brilliantly coloured embroidered head-dresses in the traditions of her native island, the jackets and aprons stiff with silken threads. With them were laid the elaborate ballgowns George had insisted she should have during her years as his wife, gowns suitable to his wealth and station. With dried rose petals scattered between the folds, they were placed in the great presses of her rooms, and my father hammered in the nails that sealed the doors of her chambers, so that he should not be tormented by her empty dresses, sad ghosts that had once held her living, breathing body within them, silks and satins that were moulded to her shape and impregnated with her scents.

And they locked away the fantastic jewels which she had brought with her, and with which I had played as a child, jewels modest in value but extravagantly rich in design and imagination. There were chryselephantine beasts, ivory creatures with gold heads or wings, leopards and griffins, set with amber eyes. There was a brooch in the form of a ship with mother-of-pearl sails and golden threads for the ship's cables, and cloak pins in the shape of dolphins leaping from pearl-studded waves, of birds with red-enamelled wings. These were the Greek jewels of the Malfine women, filigree chains from which swung mermaids with opals for their breasts and green-gilt tails, and there were lustrous deformed baroque pearls in oyster shells with silver cherubs riding on top of them. These I played with as a child, threading them into my mother's dark hair by firelight.

What else did I remember? A pendant showing an ivory huntsman with a golden bow slung over his shoulder, who stroked the head of a crouching lion, tamed by the huntsman's magic. "A great hero, Ambrose," said my mother as I took that piece in my hands, feeling the heavy warmth of the ivory and the delicately chiselled lines of the beast's mane. "A hero and a god."

And there had been a marvellous jewelled fruit, which I loved to spin round and around like a globe on its silver chain. This had been a gift to Eurydice's mother from a Greek priest, the Metropolitan of Caesarea, and was a piece of the most exquisite Byzantine workmanship. Imagine a pomegranate with the outer skin cut away, to reveal an interior of garnet seeds, set in a round honeycomb of silver. The garnets flashed a purplish red, like glistening drops of blood, as the pendant whirled around in the light.

For my mother's maid, a simple soul, all these jewels had their own purposes. "This is Cretan agate. Look at it and learn, little Ambrose. It will cure all pains in the head and the lungs. And here is cornelian, which restrains anger. And this little tree here, with peach-coloured branches, this is coral, from under the sea. Coral fortifies the heart. You must wear a piece of coral if you are in danger of losing blood from a wound."

I remembered her words, years later, under the scorching sun of Greece. I bent over a wounded man, pulled open his shirt to look for signs of life, and found a coral hand tied around his throat, I suppose by some woman like my mother's maid who had kissed and embraced him before he went away to fight. His life's blood lay drained away in a great pool at his side.

There was a remedy for everything in my mother's jewel box. There had even been a remedy for snakebite, I think— jasper, was it? And cures for all ills of the soul also, for jealousy, for lost love. A little phial of water from a fountain in Cairo, a phial of rock crystal, carved with hieroglyphs and stoppered with jade. "That is water from the Lovers' Fountain," said my mother, laughing. "No, it does not make you fall in love—quite the opposite. If you have a terrible love for someone, you must drink it and it will cure you of love. Love is a disease, you see—but it can be cured!" And she put the phial away in a leather case, specially made to keep it safe.

But one jewel she gave me to keep, a strange thing for a child, a long and snaggled tooth, brown with age, set in a heavy gold ring.

"This is the tooth of a wolf cub, little Ambrose. One of our ancestors took two cubs from a cave in Crete, after killing their mother. He tried to rear them, and with one he succeeded and it followed him like a dog. The other died, and he had its teeth set into rings for the boys of our family to wear. This you will wear later, for it is too big for you now, but you may keep it round your neck until your hand has grown large enough for it."

My father sometimes teased my mother and said that she kept me too much in the women's rooms, that I should have more manly pursuits, but I had those a-plenty after her death. With the exception of that wolf's tooth ring, all those bright and glittering toys had vanished from the light into the darkness of my dead mother's rooms. Into an oak chest went the traces of her religion also, the Cretan icons, with their rows of serried angels with wings of fire. In, too, went the paintings of the Lamentation at the Tomb of Christ, which had terrified me as a child, the dead Christ with un-earthly greenish-white flesh. Was that what my mother would look like? I wondered, soon after her death, in my childish nightmares.

There were other nightmares, later, when I was a grown man, though now I realised that I had not, for several days, experienced the dreams that had come night after night in recent months. In those feverish slumbers, the boat lands again in that little bay beneath the castle which we believe deserted. We disembark, some thirty of us, splendid in white garments with brave sashes, upon that Cretan shore. The cobalt sea, lashed here and there by the fierce sun into dazzling opalescence—black, jade green, lilac, glittering white—stretches out beyond the sands.

And now the sun is beating down upon the rocks. And upon our dead and wounded, who have been left where we fell, for the soldiers were waiting for us: we have been betrayed, and trapped between the rocks and that flashing sea.

The soldiers must have their orders: the bodies are to be left where they have fallen. So we still have our garments and our boots, and the wolf's tooth ring is still upon my finger. I have it yet.

I alone, of the thirty men who embarked so bravely to fight for freedom, I, a man not of the Greeks but a stranger to these shores, I am still living, under a heap of my comrades' bodies, my head thrusting out of the sprawling heap of limbs into the sun. Through my partly opened eyelids, I can see that the enemy has posted a sentry, to keep watch over the bodies.

All day long I must lie there, unmoving, while the sentry guard changes and a new watch is posted, through the full glare of noon, and the merciless afternoon. My clothing is drenched with blood from slashing wounds, for some of the Turkish soldiers had no gunpowder, and set about their opponents with their sabres.

I do not dare even to move my tongue over my parched lips.

If I can live till dusk, till I might move under cover of darkness, then there is just a faint chance, the slightest glimmer, of life.

I lived, to relive, again and again.

CHAPTER 10

AND now I awoke, and I was home, in England once more, but I came to and realised that I awoke to a living nightmare, for I was locked here in the prison of the ice-house, with the bodies of the dead Crawshays.

The walls now struck a damp chill into my bones. What was the time of day? Several hours must have passed since I had set out from Malfine. Through the window slits, the sky was getting darker. Dusk was coming.

Outside the icehouse, things were moving in the woods. I could hear rustling, furtive sounds, scratching noises and high-pitched cries. The creatures of the night were beginning to stir about their business.

> Light thickens, and the crow
> Makes wing to the rooky wood:
> Good things of day begin to droop and drowse,
> Whiles night's black agents to their prey do rouse.

Was the murderer who stalked in these parts, the killer of the two men who lay beside me, another of those agents of the night? How long could I remain here alive?

If a human killer did not find me, that spectral murderer, hunger, might succeed.

I looked behind me, and saw the dim white shapes outlined on their marble beds in the faint light from the window slits. Food, of a sort.

I had once talked to an outcast in Greece, a sailor, whom no man would take in his boat, a sailor who would never again go to sea.

That man had drifted, with others like himself, on a raft under the burning sun, so he told me. Held the flesh of a dead boy in his hands, a boy butchered like a calf by hungry men afloat on an empty ocean. Such things did happen at sea, yes, though pious landlubbers believed they were too dreadful even to contemplate. Is there in reality anything that is too dreadful for a man to do? I think not. That Greek sailor, for example. The meat of the boy, he had said, was hacked from the long bones by inexpert knives, and the outcast who had stared at me, crouched beside the harbour from which he would never again set sail, he had held that meat in his hands.

"But I did not eat, lord," he said to me, but even as he said it I pictured the defenceless bloody flesh held up to his cracked and dirty lips. "But I did not eat." He had said that over and over again. No one believed him. For he was alive, and the boy was dead.

The leg which I had injured in my fall began to throb monotonously. I took off my jacket and rolled it into a cushion, and then leant back against the door with the rolled-up jacket as makeshift padding.

But then, as I was contemplating the past, which had temporarily taken my mind away from this present danger in the icehouse of Malfine, I suddenly heard the sound of a footfall outside.

I climbed up to the top of the flight of steps and peered through a crack in the door. My partial view, in what was left of the light, showed something black and velvety trailing nearby.

The edge of a woman's skirt.

I let out a shout, and saw the woman start in terror, and I cursed myself as I heard her scream and saw her running away, the black skirt of her riding habit held up in her hands. It was the governess from Crawshay's, Miss Anstruther.

"It's all right! It's Ambrose Malfine! Can you get me out of here?"

She stopped her flight across the grass and turned back towards the icehouse, then slowly and cautiously she returned and I heard her fumbling with the lock.

"The key is in the lock, it's very stiff. Ah, I think I have it now."

I could see her face now as she struggled with the heavy iron key, looking white, nervous and alarmed. Then she paused and took a lace handkerchief out of a side pocket in the tightly fitted black habit, and held it up to her mouth and coughed and gasped into it. I realised that the odour of the dead men had reached her nostrils: I myself had grown accustomed to it during my imprisonment there, so that I had almost ceased to notice it.

"I am so sorry, Miss Anstruther—this must be dreadful for you."

She made no reply, but put the handkerchief away, held her head high and turned back to struggle with the key again. I heard her panting for breath, so close was she to me, just separated by the wood: the sound was oddly sexual; we might have been sharing the same pillow and gasping together in excitement.

At last there came the sound of the key scraping round in the lock and the door swung open. I fell out into the blessed, blessed air.

For several minutes I could see nothing; even the fading light of evening splintered and danced in my eyes. Gradually,

my vision adjusted to the light. I realised she was supporting
me by the elbow, as I swayed to and fro.

"I'll be all right in a moment. Just need to get my eyes
accustomed to the change."

"What happened?"

Her voice was low and controlled, though I felt her body
shaking a little.

"I was locked in—I can only suppose it was an accident.
I don't know who it was—probably some meddler who
thought the door should not be left open and decided to
turn the key in the lock! Very fortunate indeed for me that
you came along, Miss Anstruther."

She passed the lace handkerchief to me. Automatically, I
rubbed it over my face, and I suddenly realised that I must
present a grotesque sight. My scarred face was now covered
with the filth of a charnel house; my clothes were streaked
with dirt from my failed attempts to reach the windows. I
looked down at my hands. They were cut and bleeding. My
trouser leg was ripped where I had torn it on a jagged edge
of marble, and my shirt front was smeared with a green
slime. Her little handkerchief was black with dirt and I
thrust it into my pocket.

"By your leave, miss, I must attend to its laundry for you.
I am afraid I must present a most sorry sight. I believe there
is a stream in the wood just yonder—I should like to clean
myself up a little, if you would excuse me."

"I will walk with you—why, you cannot proceed alone,
sir, you are near fainting!"

It was true that as I tried to make my way to the blessed,
cool water of the stream, I staggered on my injured leg and
had to allow her to help me. If I could but have a drink of
that clean water and remove some of this muck from my
person, I might be able to make my own way back to the
house without being propped up by a woman in this humil-
iating fashion. But I must drink, wash and rest first.

We entered the wood, and my vision was clear now. I
could see that her hair, which had come down out of its pins,

and fell over my arm as she supported me, was gleaming a satiny reddish-brown in the dappled evening light that filtered through the leaves. I stepped ahead, away from her supporting arm, and led the way to a little clearing that I remembered from my childhood. Yes, the stream was still running, even in this dry summer, though it was reduced to a shallow trickle. But it splashed along between grassy banks, bright green and moist. This stream never ran dry, even in the hottest of summers. There must be an underground source somewhere in the hills behind us. The silvery-grey willow leaves flickered above the water and dragonflies of a brilliant peacock blue flitted over the surface.

I pulled her little handkerchief from my pocket and rubbed my hands with it, and then, kneeling at the side of the stream, I cupped the water in my hands and drank, like a wild man.

She turned suddenly away from me.

"I believe, sir, that your leg is quite badly injured. I can fetch my mare when you have rested a little, and she can carry you back to Malfine."

"I assure you I could not permit that, madam—I will be quite well enough to walk home."

She turned and looked at me.

It seemed somehow quite natural that she should kneel down on the grass beside me, and, quite unselfconsciously, she helped me remove my torn and dirty shirt.

I saw her eyes move over my body. I was lean and wiry, my body thin, muscled from the riding and walking at night that were my chief exertions, but across my breast ran the great fresh sabre scar that puckered the flesh and descended from my left shoulder to my navel.

"I fought in Greece," I said. "For Greek independence, to free Greece from Turkish rule. I was fortunate."

She said nothing.

I rose, moved back to the stream and splashed water over my chest and arms, and then turned back to her. She got to her feet suddenly, and reached out, touching my left shoulder, and traced the deep scar gently and slowly down the length of my chest with the trailing fingers of her hand. I knelt, still, stirring.

Suddenly she pulled her fingers away as if my skin were on fire, as if it scorched her.

Was it the close contact with death that gave me those imaginings, this carnal lust for life, that had not been awakened since I had been healed of my wounds? There were accounts of the city of Naples during the plague that had beset it, accounts that had described men and women, like things possessed, coupling in the cemeteries, on the graves, in the open tombs of the newly dead, copulating naked as the plague pits brimmed over with bodies: the graveyards full of splayed thighs and buttocks, some mottled with plague spots, some living, some dead, some scarcely alive yet still moving their limbs in a last parody of lust.

But what woman would not be appalled? I was newly emerged from a charnel house, still stinking and filthy. And she? Perhaps I imagined what I saw in her eyes.

Abruptly, I pulled myself away and turned back to the water.

I spoke over my shoulder, as I washed.

"You will ride your mare and I will walk beside you. My horse is at some little distance from here."

We walked back to the patient mare.

I knelt and locked my hands so that the governess could put her foot into my intertwined fingers and swing herself up on to the mare's back. She rode astride, like a proper horsewoman, not side-saddle in that mincing, affected way of the daughters of the local gentry. She had black glacé kid riding boots, of the very finest quality, and there was a froth of black silk petticoats as her gown swung out. Was she in mourning for the Crawshays? If so, she was dressed far more like a woman of means than a humble governess—as I had noticed before, when I had met her at the farm. There was indeed a mystery about this creature. Should I let her keep it?

We made our way slowly back to Malfine, not speaking. She did not look directly at me again, and I took the mare's bridle and led her along the paths. I did not turn my head to look at the woman in the saddle and she said nothing at all. If she felt any aesthetic admiration for the architecture of Malfine, she restrained it, and made no comment as the classical façade of the house came into view.

We reached the edge of the wood in silence, and I untethered Zaraband, who thrust her soft nose at me. I opened the gate of the rustic bridge for the horses, mounted Zaraband, and we skirted the lawn side by side on horseback to reach the house.

Once in the hall, I summoned Belos, who looked with horror at my disreputable appearance.

"I've had an accident, Belos. Would you show Miss Anstruther into the library and bring some tea?"

I turned to the woman. "Would you like something stronger? Perhaps some cognac?"

Still silence. She shook her head.

"Then a dish of tea, Belos, if you please. I'll go and clean myself up."

She put up a hand to smooth her hair, which was escaping, disordered, down her neck, and I thought that she seemed uncomfortable, confused, and added:

"Madam, I forget my manners—no doubt you would like to refresh yourself and rest. Allow me to show you, Miss Anstruther, the way to Miss Ariadne's old room."

"Miss Ariadne?" said the governess, with a questioning inflexion in her voice.

"Yes, my sister. I grant you her name sounds absurd in the depths of the English countryside—quite outlandish, is it not? But you see, my mother gave her the name."

"And what was your mother called?"

I hesitated for a moment. I had not spoken my mother's name for many years.

"Eurydice."

It sounded strangely in my mouth.

"My mother, you see, was Greek. I am what the gypsies call a *zingaro*—a man of mixed blood."

She did not babble with questions, as many women might have done at this information, but seemed to accept my exotic heredity quietly and without fuss.

We mounted the great staircase that curved above the hall, with its curling-tongued wrought-iron banister that cast sharp black arabesques of shadow upon the white walls, and her riding habit trailed its black skirt from marble step to marble step.

"My mother's rooms are shut up, but my sister's room is, I believe, suitable to receive a lady, though you may find some of the fittings a trifle outmoded. Ariadne has not been back to Malfine for many years."

I called over my shoulder to Belos, who was standing in the hall watching us ascend the stairs.

"Belos, fetch Miss Anstruther some hot water there. And bring a can of hot water to my dressing room as well, would you?"

I opened the door of Ariadne's room and Elisabeth went in, murmuring her thanks. I called after her. I think now that I did not want her to vanish from my sight.

"Your account of the events at Crawshay's will be needed. Perhaps you could describe what you discovered there—if, of course, you feel strong enough when you come downstairs."

There was an assenting murmur from within the room. I shut the door gently.

Needing a drink, I went downstairs, entered my library and poured a tot of brandy from the tantalus that stood on the table. This was the only room in the house that was kept in order. Around me were the familiar long bookshelves, fronted with gilded grilles, behind which the leather bindings, rich calf with gold-lettered spines, gleamed like long jewels in the sunlight, amber, dark green, carnelian, topaz. They reminded me of my mother's jewels.

Once, in that country of the past, truth and justice had

meant something to me—something I had forgotten and
thought buried. But when Elisabeth Anstruther had touched
that sabre scar, had traced the line it had carved in my flesh
on that distant shore, had she rekindled the dying spark of an
almost-expired passion? The dumb animal suffering of that
wretched gypsy, and then the cool touch of her hand—what
had they revived?

I had almost dozed off, sitting there in the warm library.
It was late evening, I realised. The whole episode, the imprisonment in the icehouse, the terrible swoop of lust beside
the stream, the silent return, had taken several hours.

Then I started wondering. Why had Elisabeth Anstruther
been there, near the icehouse, in the first place? It was out of
the way, deserted. An unlikely place for her to stray towards,
so far from Crawshay's. I pulled out the strands of hair I had
taken from the body of old Crawshay, the strands that had
been caught round one of his buttons.

They were long chestnut hairs: Elisabeth Anstruther's,
beyond a doubt. That part of her story seemed true, then:
she had acquired the blood on her gown innocently enough:
as she had bent over the old man and tried to find some vestiges of life in him, some strands of hair had become entangled with the button. If she was telling the truth then all
pointed to an outsider, perhaps the crippled stranger skulking round the village, as a possible murderer.

I made my way up the sweeping curve of the staircase to
my room, the master bedroom at the top of the stairs. Here
was my dressing closet, a bath, fitted with mahogany and
brass, and a washstand on which a copper can bounded with
brass was steaming with hot water, where Belos had set it
down according to instructions. I washed, changed my
shirt, felt human again.

And yet something still troubled me. There was something I had wanted to ask Elisabeth Anstruther about. There
was a weightier problem, but it did not seem related to the
murders at the farm; my brain felt as if it were whirling still,
after the danger of the morning, and I endeavoured to focus

my attention on the immediate question which presented itself.

Yes, that was it. Why had she been at the icehouse? What was she looking for? I had never asked her that simple question.

I opened the door of my room, hesitated, then stepped out and across the landing to my sister's room—or rather, the room that had been used by my sister until she chose never to return to Malfine, but to stay in London with distant relatives, pillars of respectability who could give her the solid security and the respectable society she would never find in her father's decaying mansion.

I knocked on the door.

There was no response.

The door was not tight shut and I pushed it open. The Indian muslin curtains fluttered in the breeze.

The room was empty.

CHAPTER 11

I, Ambrose Malfine, am a rational animal, an admirer of the philosopher Voltaire, but, like Voltaire, I know that perfectly rational beings may have difficulties in existing in the real, and utterly unreasonable, world and that illogical impulses are constantly intruding. I am aware, therefore, of my own admixture of concerns in my enquiries into the Crawshay murders, and I readily admit that I include the papers that follow for reasons that go beyond their relevance to the case. They are, most certainly, an important part of the accumulation of evidence, for they form part of a vital testimony. I had heard an account from Marie Crawshay, I had heard the version of the accused gypsy, but I had received no record of Elisabeth Anstruther's story. It therefore forms an additional portion of the history of the deadly events at the farm, for it is told by one who was part of that household and knew its intimate secrets, one who was an intelligent observer of the passions that were hidden to outsiders—and one who became herself embroiled in the events that followed upon those powerful emotions.

But I will confess that this document stirred within me feelings and desires that sat ill at ease with the reasoned chain of logic that I endeavoured to apply, for I must confess that I experienced emotions of intrigue and attraction towards the writer, sensations that made me cast an eye over the copperplate handwriting with more than usual interest.

I have them still, these foolscap pages of fine linen paper, and, as I touch them, I fancy I feel her hand brushing against mine as it skims across a line, dips the quill in the ink, and again moves back and forth, setting down this narrative in her clear and elegant script.

I am very frightened, though I try not to show it. I have left your house—left your protection, I sense—and I am sending these papers to you, the only human being that I can trust. You will see that I have set down everything that I learned about the Crawshays during my stay at the farm. I know there have been many rumours about me and I desire to dispel the mysteries: you will find here the truth of my own life story.

You asked for my account of what happened at the farmhouse. Forgive my feelings: I could not so soon face you, after our encounter, and prefer to set it out on paper so that no present feelings may intrude into this record.

I write in secret, having locked myself into my room at Crawshay's farm, fearing discovery, for ever since I came into this house I have had the uneasy sense of being watched. Tom Granby, the man you stationed here, is downstairs, and I believe him to be an honest man, both from his countenance and from his discourse, but there is something in this farmhouse that is very clever, in a certain way, too clever for the Tom Granbys of this world. I am afraid it will outwit him.

Here it is then, my story, the history told by an insider, the tale that ends in murder. In a sense, it is a secret family history, not the official record that is usually committed to paper, for it is women's history: things that passed between Marie and myself as we talked or worked within the house,

things that women confide in each other, with the under-
standing that they are not for the ears of the menfolk.

Perhaps I am breaking faith in a way, though I have
sworn no oath to keep these things private. Nevertheless, the
crimes committed here were so frightful that I feel I am jus-
tified in breaking confidences and betraying them to you. And
also, I must own, I sense that you understand the conversa-
tion of women, know what is important to us and what af-
fects us. I think you have a sympathy for our sex which is not
usual amongst English gentlemen—perhaps it is because of
your Greek ancestry.

I shall get this sent over by Mattie, who cannot read.
Keep or destroy it, Lord Ambrose, as you wish.

The Crawshays had once been a prosperous family, or so I
understand, and I must begin with something of their story,
which has become so enmeshed with mine. They were not
gentry, but they were "well set up," as people say in these
parts of those who have a comfortable sufficiency, of solid
burghers or respectable farmers who own their land.

But old Crawshay's rule ruined the family. His workmen
left the farm, because they would not take the lash of his
tongue when he was sober, nor the blows of his fists when he
was drunk. Tenants were reluctant to bring in their rents,
and be abused for their pains. Fields were neglected, sheds,
stores and cottages became dilapidated, nettles grew in the
fields and the cattle looked lean.

Marie, whom you have met, my lord, was the daughter of
an alehouse keeper in the next village. Her father's business
had some pretensions to being an inn, but it had nevertheless accustomed her to hard work and rough behaviour,
which was good preparation for life at Crawshay's.

The match with Edmund should have been a step up for
her. After I, Elisabeth Anstruther, came to Crawshay's as
governess to Marie's son, I heard many stories from Marie of
the days before her marriage, of the beaux she might have
married, of the days when young men rode from miles

around to the alehouse to court the landlord's pretty daughter. She must have been a beauty as a young girl, and the evidence for that is still in her face, in spite of all that has since happened to her.

Edmund Crawshay had seemed a real catch for the landlord's daughter, so I understand. At that time, things at Crawshay's had not declined so badly, and the farm was one of the biggest in the district. Edmund was the old man's only child, and the inheritance would fall to him in due course.

Marie pictured herself in charge of all her domain, the mistress of a prosperous farmhouse, with servants for the rough work. After the old man died, the farm could easily be brought up again, by dint of good management.

Edmund was in the full flush of his good looks. He had that fair-haired handsomeness often found in the English countryside, blond locks and corkscrews of hair, an open, ruddy face, and an easy charm of manner that must have been entirely natural to him, for he certainly did not learn it from his father, and his mother had been long dead.

I have to picture him in their courting days, as Marie described him to me, for when I came to meet him first, he had already declined: his pink cheeks were red-veined pads of flesh, his hair was usually darkened with grease or perspiration, and he was generally showing signs of the decline into sottishness that was overwhelming him: he would go the same way as his father, I thought often and enough. Nevertheless, as I have said, when he went courting Marie, he must have been the catch of the neighbourhood, and a most beauteous young man.

But above all, I think, she saw that he was pliable. She did not, of course, express it quite like this in her talks with me, but I understood her to have perceived that particular weakness in Edmund, with a kind of penetrative shrewdness which she possesses—not intellect, perhaps, but she has a way of grasping certain things about people very quickly. Or rather, she formerly had this ability: she too is now sadly declined. In fact, that handsome young couple who were wed ten years ago has disappeared unrecognisably: both of them, bride and groom, have had their minds destroyed by that wicked old man. Edmund has lost his life, and I almost feel it would be better for Marie if she had perished with him.

But when she met Edmund, she was attracted by his very softness, for she understood that she would have her own way after their marriage. She used some words such as "I knew he would always respect my wishes," or "He would never have me running about at his beck and call, of that I was certain, before our marriage." She, by force of personality, would be the dominant partner, and she knew it. Under Marie's pretty exterior, there were ambitions, you may be sure.

Ambitions that were thwarted by old Crawshay.

In the early days of their marriage, he had not appeared to be an obstacle, for he seemed dreadfully old to her then. With the optimism of youth, callous but innocent, she thought he must die soon, and then her Edmund would come into his own.

But somehow he kept his strength from year to year; it seemed rather to grow, in spite of his drinking bouts, the gross dinners with which he regaled himself, the way in which he would ride through rain and storm for a wager and fall into bed in wet clothes and riding boots. The old man was like a tree; thick-chested, strong-thighed, with black bushes for his eyebrows. His face was weatherbeaten into a kind of leather: he seemed inhuman, indestructible.

And Marie now perceived that Edmund's weakness was fatal. She could not persuade him to challenge his father over anything. That was something she had not considered—if Edmund was feeble, it was because his father had made him so. He had long ago broken his son and demolished his pride, as he had demolished Edmund's mother, who had once argued with her husband and found herself bruised and shaking on the stone flags of the farmhouse with blood on her mouth. She had never again attempted to challenge him. It was Edmund's mother, I believe, who brought the piano, and that pretty parlour chair, those small luxuries, into the harsh old house. What pathetic relics they now seem, reminders of her charms and hopes!

Marie herself had always refused to crawl to her father-in-law, and the old man was induced to treat her with some respect. She said that her father would always have her back if he thought his daughter were misused, and he would not see her mistreated. She threatened Crawshay with reprisals if he should offer her any violence. It is more likely that he was amused by her defiance, than deterred by her threats, for he certainly would not have shrunk from a fight. But he would have other ways of breaking her to his will. I can see him, with those deep-set eyes, the upper lids drooping down, contemplating her, waiting for some chance to master her, some way of gaining absolute dominance over the one being who dared challenge him. It was his way to study his victims: I know, for I was one.

Marie had kept table at home after her mother had died, and was an excellent housekeeper: her desire for gentility made her maintain her domain in good order, and she had learned the art of catering for large country appetites. In the little dining room and the parlour, which Crawshay and Edmund had never used, the tables which had been unpolished since the death of Edmund's mother now gleamed with beeswax polish. Silver that had lain black and tarnished in cupboards was taken out and brought to a glitter with jeweller's rouge, ordered expressly from Callerton for Mistress Crawshay. Pantry shelves were filled with preserves and bottled fruit. Linen, old but fine, was shaken out of the presses, and the worn sheets and pillowcases on which the male Crawshays had been content to lie were consigned to make dust sheets and floor cloths.

Crawshay dispensed with the services of the old woman who had kept house for them before Edmund's marriage. After all, he reasoned, Marie had the services of the girl,

Mattie, who came up from the village to help her with the floor-scrubbing and the laundry. What more did she need?

A kind of truce thus prevailed between the two of them, old Crawshay and Marie; each knew the other's strengths and values, each assessed the battle lines. Edmund was a pawn between them, and one day they would fight for control of him. He was terrified of his father, but passionate for his wife; in bed Marie knew that, as her husband panted and thrust away over her slim body, so her influence was secure.

The birth of her son should have settled the balance decisively in Marie's favour. She would have the prestige that accrued to the mother of a male heir: she was no longer a young girl whose wishes might be flouted as of no consequence whatever, but a matron.

Yet in this very event that should have seen Marie's ascendancy, old Crawshay found his leverage to destroy her.

Lord Ambrose, false modesty and simpering hints can have no place in this account. I am simply a gentlewoman, and I reckon it better breeding to be plain about the matters whereof I must now speak than to flutter with genteel embarrasment.

Let me set it down boldly, therefore. Young Edmund's birth was very difficult. Marie, who is a slender woman, had the narrowest of passages for the birth of a baby that the midwife had ever seen. She was in labour for two whole days; the physician was fetched, and cut her with his instruments, but not enough for the head of the child to come through, and she was dreadfully torn and lacerated when at last young Edmund forced his bawling way into the world.

Afterwards, the pain was excruciating. She lay in bed, scarcely able to move. She had lost a great deal of blood, but the midwife had managed to staunch the bleeding, packing poultices of some herb into her torn flesh. Yet the pains continued.

Edmund was patient at first, but a while later they tried again until at last he moved away, then got up and left their bedroom. So on all following occasions, the experience was repeated, husband and wife despairing separately as her body fought against his demands.

Marie told me that, one night, he did not come to their bedroom at all.

The next day, when she went down in the morning, the Crawshays, father and son, were seated at the dining table. Edmund was nursing his head, and turning his face away from her. She saw that his eyes were bloodshot and fumes of stale wine rose from his body. He scarcely seemed to dare look at her. There was something else mingled with the wine, an odour of some cheap perfume, patchouli or something unfamiliar.

She looked at the old man, and caught him unawares. He was staring at her with triumph in his eyes.

He knew. Beyond a shadow of a doubt, he knew how things lay between husband and wife. And now Edmund had left her bed and gone whoring—probably his father had encouraged him in it. For she had lost her chief weapon in the warfare for possession of Edmund the pawn. He could get his pleasure elsewhere.

Marie slept alone for the next fortnight, but she did not despair. She was but in retreat, not vanquished—she thought and plotted for her future and that of her child.

She sent a message to the midwife.

"Laudanum," said the druggist in Callerton, to whom Marie sent me for fresh supplies of the medicine which she had been taking since then. She asked me not to mention my visit to that particular shop to anyone, but said that she had a private need for certain medicaments, and she was so glad now that I had come to Crawshay's as governess, and would perhaps be able from time to time to help her in little ways.

"Oh, many a gentlewoman takes it in such a case, I assure you," said the druggist. "It helps with certain—how shall I put it—helps to cope with certain demands that are made on a lady from time to time—demands made by her husband . . . and it is not in any way injurious—I always recommend it myself in such cases . . ."

"It was suggested to Mistress Crawshay, I believe, by old Kezia Hannington, who attended her at the birth of her child . . ."

"Oh yes, well, they are giving up their pots and herbs, these old creatures—their country medicines. Laudanum is a real remedy, not some old wives' tale, I assure you, Miss Anstruther. Oh yes, I know your name—everyone in the district knows the Crawshay household. What a handsome young son Mistress Crawshay has, your charge Master Edmund—my, what a fine fellow he will grow up to be! Thank you, ma'am, I have wrapped it up, you see, and the instructions are on the bottle, but Mistress Crawshay will know what to do. I guarantee, it is an end to . . . how may I put it with delicacy to an unmarried lady such as yourself . . . an end to marital . . . disharmony. And I always have a little supply in stock, so don't fear to ask me when Mistress Crawshay next requires some."

The druggist spoke the truth, in his dark little shop. Within the fluted blue bottle Marie found ease and relief from pain, joy and light and the sweetness of most lovely dreams, as she described them.

After a little sip from her first magic bottle of laudanum, Marie was laughing, floating, drowsy. After some experimenting with the delicious juice, the sweet double decoction of opium wrapped up in brandy, she called Edmund into her room one afternoon. She was coy with the details as she re-told them to me, but did not spare her hints, for I fancy she might have taken a certain pleasure in the recounting of them.

That afternoon, Edmund found his wife lying in their great oak bed, and she was laughing as she sat up to greet him, naked under the covers. Her eyes were unafraid of pain and she reached out to him in the old way, the way she had before Edmund was born and all the difficulties had started.

For a few moments, it seemed to Marie that Edmund hesitated. Perhaps he feared that this was all on the surface, that she would not really have become her old self again, that there would be the shrinking and weeping as before. But he climbed into bed beside her, and mounted on top of her, and there was the same joyous old way that he remembered, and she intimated to me that he was almost tearful with relief at having got his wife back.

Over the next few weeks, their life seemed to have resumed its old patterns, except that her appetite appeared to have vanished. As I observed when I came to stay at the farm, she picked at her food and grew hollow under the eyes. Sometimes she broke out into clammy sweats, and sometimes she wept for no reason at all. But the demon between her legs that had barred her husband's way, that had vanished—there was no doubt about it.

And old Crawshay, I believe, old Crawshay saw the subtle changes in manner between the two, the way in which Edmund did not fear to give his wife a small caress in public, the closeness with which she leant against him as they mounted the stairs, and knew that in the battle for control of Edmund, Marie had regained her weapons.

CHAPTER 12

This was what I, Elisabeth Anstruther, learnt from Marie, at first partly from seeing her in the privacy of her chamber, partly from what she let fall by chance, and then, later, as she grew more desperate, what she told me outright as she begged me to get her supplies of the drug. In fact, it was for laudanum that she had sent me to Callerton on that very morning of the murders, and as I drove back in the pony-cart I had the little bottle safely tucked away in my pocket. I forgot all in the confusion of finding the bodies and it was not till Marie begged me for it after you had left that I remembered to hand it over to her.

But I must tell you how I came to be in the role of confidante to the lonely mistress of an isolated farmhouse. And will have to trust you with my history, of which nothing is known by any, save for the little that old Crawshay had gathered in the short time that I was under his roof.

I am from a very respectable family indeed, I assure your lordship, a family who would doubtless be appalled if they should discover anything of the events that have recently happened to me, and I earnestly beg that you will keep silent as to my personal history.

The Anstruthers are far too upright to be mixed up in the doings of the aristocracy, Lord Ambrose. They regard your class, the aristocrats and great land-owners, as licentious and dissipated wretches who know nothing of countinghouses, investments and the like. The Anstruthers are the kind of solid bourgeois family that positively abhors any kind of "showiness." They live in terror of flashiness, debts, gambling and all the other commonplaces of upper-class society.

In the world in which they move, solidity and stability are the chief virtues. Their wealth is solid. And it comes from one of the very few respectable aspects of trade. For some reason, the provision of drink has always been regarded as a gentlemanly occupation in England, free from the stigma associated with iron foundries or cotton mills. The great brewers and vintners have always had a respectable place in English society, and my family is from what may be regarded as the upper echelons, the cream, if one may so put it, of that trade.

The Anstruthers were wine-importers, and as such were among the untitled nobility of the West of England. They needed no further qualifications for this position than their old-established port and sherry business, where men wearing discreet coats of dark broadcloth sipped from little sample glasses in rooms panelled with fine wood.

The family home was over our business, in one of those tall houses in Bristol where the top floors received generous daylight through Georgian windows that reached practically from floor to ceiling, while the sounds of the harbour, the shouts of sailors and the bustle of loading and unloading, drifted up from the port.

It was my father who formed a connection with the French wine trade. The family fortunes had been founded a century before, importing port wine, so they had connections with Portugal and maintained a representative in

Lisbon, but French wines had never formed much of the business of the Anstruthers. By special requests, for favoured customers, they would occasionally import fine cognacs or champagnes through agents in Paris, but they preferred to concentrate on the business they knew. "A cobbler should stick to his last" was a typical Anstruther maxim.

My father was an ambitious young man, determined on expanding the business. The Napoleonic Wars had prevented regular imports from Spain and Portugal for some time, but France was beginning to recover from the effects of war, peace having been but recently established. In most parts of France, in spite of the terrible strife the country had endured, the grapes were still somehow gathered and the vintage still trodden, the great wines famed throughout Europe still produced. And, word came to the Anstruthers, the great cellars lay mostly untouched, although many châteaux might have been burnt down over the heads of their owners. Beneath them, locked behind iron grilles deep in the musty, cobwebby vaults, the wine had slumbered as battle and famine raged above, as revolution came and went, as the owners of the vineyards lost their heads on the guillotine and the starving peasants raided the fields for corn and potatoes.

There came a time when it seemed safe for an Englishman to travel discreetly in France once again, at least on such peaceable errands as the buying of merchandise. My father set out and here began a love story.

My father fell in love with the countryside of Northern France, with its moist grey-blue skies so like those of home, and its shiny countryside, bright green, dotted with brilliant red fruit and black and white cows. And little glasses of a thousand golden fluids.

On his very first visit, Henry found a cellar, which he bought from a widow living alone in the great château above it. She was more than willing to sell. Her husband and her two sons had frozen to death somewhere in a blizzard on Napoleon's Russian campaign. She had no heart to

remain in the lifeless château, which had been legally returned to her family with the restoration of the Bourbon
monarchy in France.

The contents of that cellar retailed at a handsome profit
in Bristol, and upon it my father built the fortunes of his
family, for he now felt well set up enough to marry my
mother, the daughter of a wine merchant. She came from a
solid and well-respected family similar to my father's own
relatives, and with the marriage there disappeared, I believe,
the last trace of romance or rebellion which my father had
possessed. Perhaps I have inherited some of that venture-
some spirit that motivated him as a young man.

The young couple were installed, soon after the marriage,
in one of the fashionable Bristol houses which overlooked
the Downs, in an airy and delightful part of town. They
duly proceeded to produce offspring—they "blended," as
my paternal grandfather rather tastelessly joked at the christening of their first child.

I was their third child. The first two were boys. I was
conscious from a very early age that my mother thought me
rather peculiar-looking: she never ceased to comment on
one particular feature in my face.

"La, but the child has such strange eyes!" she would say
as I sat on her lap or ran across the nursery floor. "They are
the eyes of a changeling, I do protest! No one in either of
our families has eyes of this curious colour—why, whether
they are yellow or grey or both at once one cannot tell—
they vary with every changing of the light!"

My father's family had respectable blue eyes. My
mother's were brown, pretty, round, open.

Once I heard her saying to our nurse, when she did not
think I was near, but I was in the dressing closet just out of
her bedroom, and could hear their conversation quite plainly:

"I do believe that she has yellow eyes like old
Anstruther—my husband's grandfather, that is. He was an
old rogue, you know!"

So I knew at an early age that some persons might think

me untrustworthy merely by reason of the colour of my eyes, yet I beg you to accept that I am a truthful creature and do not deceive you now.

Well, my childhood was uneventful, Lord Ambrose, save that I had a few pleasures which perhaps a child in another city might not have enjoyed. I had a marmoset for a pet, bought from a sailor. It had a jacket of red flannel, with tiny gold buttons, and I loved its little wrinkled face most faithfully and cried dreadfully when it died one raw winter, its breath wheezing in tiny coughs, for it could not withstand the harsh climate to which it had been brought.

In the mornings, my nurse would take me for a morning walk, and we would make our way sometimes down on to the quays, where we were partly frightened and partly thrilled at the shouts and sounds and the strange tongues, and the yells and laughter of the sailors. My father put a stop to this, and ordained safe and orderly strolls upon the Downs, but I had already become fascinated with what I had seen on the quays: with the spices and silks unloaded for sale, with the parakeets in cages offered for sale in the streets.

I had a gown of French lace at my christening in the church of St. Mary Redcliffe in Bristol, more fashionable than the cathedral, though I cannot say I took much note of the lace at such a tender age. My father had acquired a French representative, a man whose opinion he valued and whose friendship he wished to keep. So when it came to the christening of the first Anstruther daughter, my father asked his French friend's wife to stand godmother to his child, and, as her family were Huguenots who had clung to their faith through many centuries of persecution, there were no religious objections. Madame presented me with the gown of French lace. I was named after my grandmother, that is, my father's mother, but my name was spelt in the French way, Elisabeth, and I was given the second name of Madeleine because it was the name of my French godmother.

Madame Madeleine, as I called her, was genuinely fond of

her protégée, although the relationship had originally been dictated by the men of the two families concerned in order to make secure their business ties. I spent many summers in France, in Bordeaux, at the home of Madame Madeleine, and in their country château, and I learned to speak the language well. And I learned also one or two things about garments that English women do not know—that it is better to have as fine a quality of material as possible, even if the dress is of the simplest, and that it must be cut and sewn perfectly, no matter how ordinary the occasion when it is worn. These are matters that in England are understood only by your gentlemen's tailors, for English women are all frills and furbelows—with nothing of what Madame Madeleine would have considered style at all!

However, my lord, I am digressing from this history, with which I venture to trouble you. I learned a few things which have enabled me to earn my living, that is what I chiefly wish to say. As well as French, I picked up a fair amount of geography, for my father had a globe which he would turn to point out the places that the wine merchants spoke of. Angoulême, Rheims, and further afield, Lisbon, Jamaica, Madeira, the Bay of Biscay. Monemvasia, where Malmsey wine came from. Ratafia, the sweet wine we sipped with tiny macaroon biscuits.

So I have the accomplishments of a lady, and a few more besides. Gradually, we spent more and more time in France. My mother had rheumatism (sometimes as the mists crept up the Avon, and she sat in her boudoir in the Bristol house, the pain of her aching joints creasing her pretty face, I thought of my poor little marmoset) and she felt the climate in France was better for her. My brothers loved the riding and hunting in the great forests that were stocked with boar and deer. Our family eventually rented a house in France and spent most of the year there, though when the boys were of school age they were sent to study in England, and my father had to make frequent visits to Bristol for business reasons.

There was a tendency, one which is always apparent in any group of exiles, for the little community of English families in the Bordeaux district to cohere, clinging together as if to form a mutual defence against the outside world. And of this community my own family formed a respected though occasional part. They were invited to the dinners, to the hare-coursing, to the balls and the sketching parties that made up the amusements of their fellow countrymen.

And out of this arose that folly which entrapped me, a madness which seized me and which I have regretted ever since. That madness is the reason for my appearance here, stranded in the English countryside, in the home of the Crawshays. But it has nothing to do with the matter immediately in hand, which is the murder of the Crawshays, father and son, and I will spare you the story of a very foolish young woman. Sufficient to say that old Crawshay found me in a desperate situation; I had little choice but to accept his offer, to go as governess to his grandson. He believed I was quite alone, that I had no family living. In a sense, that was true.

Just as, in a way, the rumours of the country folk, that Crawshay bought me at the fair, these are true also, for I had no choice but to go with him, if I was not to starve. I sold myself into servitude for food and a roof over my head.

Edmund and Marie Crawshay asked no awkward questions. Picture the scene. The old man has been away at the fair. They know his caprice, what a drunkard he is, how he will indulge any whim when he wants to, if he wants to. He has announced he will get some respectable servant who can read and write to help Marie in the house. Marie will teach the boy his manners and his letters, until he is of age to go away to school.

This was already discussed and decided between them, as little Edmund grew out of the baby stage of existence.

"I must have a servant," she told him. "I cannot do all the

work here and teach the child at the same time. He is beginning to run wild like a little savage and it is not right that he should learn nothing."

"I'll have no servants living in the house here! They're nothing but a pack of thieves and troublemakers—servants, indeed!" said Crawshay, as she had known he would.

"He is your grandson!" Marie riposted. "How is he to be brought up? Like the calves and piglets, I suppose. Like an animal!"

Crawshay would have been holding a glass of brandy in his hand. His dirty boots, stinking of the farmyard midden, staying quarrelsome on his feet until he fell, stupefied, over his bed.

"The child's well enough!" he growled.

"He can't grow up like this. You know that well enough. He's entitled to something."

Crawshay damned the expense, and he damned the nuisance, but he must have known that Marie was right. Somewhere in his malicious old brain, he knew that he could not let his grandson fall into the condition of an illiterate labourer. As Marie had calculated, the old man still possessed some vestiges of family pride. Some schooling the boy must have, some traces of education. The remains of the gentleman's schooling he had received still hung around Crawshay himself like a ghostly coat of tattered velvet, dirty and dissolute as he was. The boy was his own flesh and blood and entitled to take his place in the world. The Crawshays might be mere farmers, but still, they were masters of servants, not servile themselves.

Marie's victory was not total. Crawshay made one condition and she had to give way to it.

"I'll pick her myself. I'll have no servant under my roof who's not of my own choosing."

He chose me.

CHAPTER 13

My lord, I ask you to do as I have done, and to picture the scene in the farmhouse just before my arrival. What will the old man bring home? Will he have hired some draggle-tailed maidservant, dirty and drunk as her master? Will he have closed at a shrewd price for the Crawshay cattle and then squandered it with the women in the barn behind the Badger's Head, the lowest drinking den in Callerton, which was old Crawshay's preferred venue of celebration?

At last, Edmund and Marie Crawshay hear the sound of the pony and trap. The stable door creaks as the old mare is shut in for the night. Then comes the light of the lantern crossing the yard. The parlour door opens, and Crawshay pushes me into the room, where I am blinking in the lamplight, and Edmund and Marie can scarce believe their eyes. Crawshay cackles.

"I found you a governess. A proper governess."

He is delighted with himself, in high good humour, pleased with his amazing nose for a bargain, with his capacity to astonish his family. Marie has never seen him in such good spirits.

It was too late at night for questions. I was given the room intended for a maid, with a high and narrow little iron bed, a pitcher, a washstand and a hook behind the door for hanging my dress. Nothing more had been considered necessary. Later, the old man told Marie to give me one of the principal bedrooms. It annoyed her, as he no doubt intended it should.

Old Crawshay would only laugh when people tried to find out how he had come by his "bargain governess." That was a secret between him and me, and, astonishingly, it remained a secret. He kept silent, not out of any respect or sensitivity towards my feelings, but because he loved to tease and puzzle, and the whole thing gave him a new lease on life, keeping people guessing. And so they created their own story about me, the tale that he had actually bought me at the fair. In a way, it is true; I had to sell my labour, like any servant, for food on my plate and a roof over my head. I went with Crawshay because there was nowhere else to go, just as if he had indeed bought me. Where there is no choice but to starve, is there any choice at all? That was my opinion then, and that was why I agreed to go with the old man to this remote farmhouse in a district where I knew not a single soul, and I beg you, my lord, not to think too badly of my motives.

As for Edmund and Marie, I do not think they really cared where the governess had come from, and indeed, my lord, I do assure you it has nothing to do with the terrible events which have occurred at the farm. My past life is my past life, and let us say no more about it.

Sufficient to say, I stayed. And I witnessed the comings and goings of the gypsies—of the man who now lies in the dungeons deep underground beneath your mansion of Malfine.

I did not understand why the gypsy and his woman were allowed by Crawshay to draw their caravan, pulled by a horse with ribs sticking out like the staves of a broken barrel, into one of his fields. I would have expected him to drive off the newcomers with blows and curses. But I did not know then the old man's terrible perversity of temperament. The gypsies were allowed to stay on his land, not through any touch of kindness in the old man's breast, but because they irritated his neighbours out of their skins. They were, I suspect, in the same position as I found myself at the farm: favoured by Crawshay in order to annoy others. The gypsies thieved from the village? So much the better, so long as they did not thieve from Crawshay's farm (and they did not—as far as I know, they never took so much as a straw from their benefactor). They poached from the squire? All to the good, as far as Crawshay was concerned—as long as they did not snare a single rabbit on Crawshay land. The villagers might complain, the gentry fume—the more they did so, the better Crawshay liked his unorthodox tenants.

The man from the gypsy caravan was given work in the fields during the harvest. He began to call at the farmhouse every day, as the light faded and the farm hands left the fields.

I watched Marie in her kitchen the first day the gypsy came. He stopped and looked at her through the doorway, hesitating like a dog on the threshold. He was covered in a fine dust; sweat still stood on his head and neck and there was an earthy smell that drifted in with him, not unpleasant, somehow, not a dirty smell at all, just—animal.

"Are you thirsty?" asked Marie, and he nodded. She went to the pump over the stone sink, but then Crawshay came in and saw what she was doing.

"Give him milk," he said.

So Marie fetched the pitcher. The gypsy drank, tipping his head right back and pouring the milk into his throat, like a white stream. And every day after that he would stop at the kitchen door and Marie gave him a pitcher of milk or cider. She always watched him while he drank; when he had finished he wiped his mouth delicately.

I do not know why old Crawshay favoured him in this particular way: there was some game he was playing with the gypsy and Marie, I have no doubt of it. All this summer, the farmhouse was a house filled with watchers: Marie looking at the gypsy as he tipped the pitcher to his lips and drank, and Crawshay watching the both of them from the passage door, as if he had some purpose of his own, as if they were flies already caught and struggling in a web.

But perhaps they resisted his toils, perhaps they were not puppets after all, Marie, Edmund, the gypsy. I believe that I, too, was at one time one of his puppets, and that he desired to make me dance to his tune. It would be true to say, my lord, that we all hated him; we would all, Edmund, Marie, myself, have cheerfully seen him dead; any of us might have killed him. And not only at the farm—I'm sure there were many in these parts who had cause to hate the old man, for he was a violent and contemptuous creature, forever making enemies, there's no doubt about it. But as for poor harmless Edmund, why, I know that I myself did not kill him, and I cannot think why Marie should have become the murderess of her devoted husband, nor of anyone else who ever bore a grudge against him, so that lends colour to the villagers' supposition that they, Edmund and his father, were indeed done to death by the gypsy.

Nevertheless, I observed the pattern of life at Crawshay's this last month, during the harvest. So you see, what I wish to say is this—that I do not believe the gypsy would have killed old Crawshay. Why should he? Crawshay was his only benefactor. No one else in the district would even have allowed him to settle his caravan on their land. They say the man killed the Crawshays, both of them, in order to steal the watch and a few guineas from the old man—but, as I say, in their dealings with Crawshays, the gypsy and his wife never touched a thing that was not freely given to them.

So when I returned to the farm yesterday after I had been to the town of Callerton, and heard Marie screaming in the house as the pony and cart entered the yard, it did not cross my mind that the gypsy had been involved in anything.

I could not make out what Marie was saying at first—something about the pistols and the old man. I ran into the house and saw them there, slumped around the table, the blood pouring out.

It was an appalling sight. There was blood and brains spattered all round them, and splinters of bone and teeth near Edmund, whose jaw was almost carried away by a bullet. I saw immediately that Edmund could have no life left in him. But I could not believe the old man was dead—it was as if a monster had been slain there, in an English farmhouse. I was still wary of him, you see, as if I feared he might come to life at any moment, might spring up and laugh or yell at me. But I forced myself to go around the table. He did not move: I crept closer till I was beside him. His head was hanging down: after a few minutes, seeing there was no movement at all, I touched the side of his cheek. Still no movement. Then I bent towards him and raised his head up and I saw then the terrible wound in his throat and the blood gushing all down his breast. Somehow, his head flopped towards me and I stumbled and fell over towards him—it was at that moment, as I struggled to regain my balance, that I got a great smear of the old man's blood across the front of my gown. I saw you observing that, my lord, when you came to Crawshay's yesterday, for one need be with you only two or three minutes to know your eyes are as sharp as a bird of prey—you are like a hawk on a perch as you sit in a room and look at a person.

There was something more—something that horrified me and made me panic and run out of the room, for my hair became entangled with him, with the buttons on his jacket I think, and he seemed to be pulling me down towards him, dead and bleeding as he was.

I tore myself away from him, my hair coming down as I did so, and I felt the pain as some strands that had caught up were torn out as I pulled away, but I cared not, for my only thought was to get away from that dreadful hold that the old creature seemed to have even in death. I ran out into the yard, where the mare still stood, and drove to the village as if the hounds of hell were behind me. I roused them to the alert, and those that were not at work in the fields came back to the farm with me; by then, Marie had calmed a little for she had taken some laudanum and it had a quietening effect upon her. She told her story to the men who came with me, and they were vehemently roused up and determined the gypsy was guilty. Some of them set off towards the clearing where his caravan is encamped, to find him, as I understand, with a bundle of linen containing those things taken from old Crawshay's body, which was interpreted as certain proof of his guilt. And then I watched from a window as they dragged him to the cart, and was horrified when I divined their purpose in tying him to the wheel. Marie would not watch. She said she cared not what they did, she must look after her child, and she sat with little Edmund, shielding him from the sounds that were coming from the yard where they had the cart set up.

The rest you know, my lord, for then you arrived, fetched by some spirits amongst the men who were less bold than their fellows, and I was never so glad to see a person in my entire life.

I feared you might have suspicions of me, for you clearly had doubts about the gypsy's guilt, and I might have been the next to be suspected of those terrible crimes. I say "terrible," but I will not be hypocritical, for the death of Edmund, who had never done any harm in his life and was like to do none as long as he lived, was indeed a heinous thing, but I cannot pretend to sorrow for the old man, as I have already said, although I may fall under suspicion of his murder.

I am, after all, an outsider here, a stranger, my history not known, and I had that telltale evidence of blood upon me, where I had bent down and touched the old man. So this evening I was on my way to Malfine to speak to you, to assure you of my innocence, and as I came along the pathway I heard sounds coming from the icehouse. I was fearful of investigating, for I knew that the bodies had been taken there to wait for the inquest, but I recognised your voice: how the door of the icehouse came to be barred on the outside, thus imprisoning you, I know not, for I saw no one else about as I neared the place. I beg you to believe my entire innocence.

CHAPTER 14

THERE was one final, and enigmatic, sentence before her signature at the bottom of the letter:

I cannot explain in any way what happened this evening.

That moment when she touched my naked flesh beside the stream and I had desired her so desperately? Was that what she meant? Had it been mutual?

I set down the bundle of papers, with their hurriedly written superscription, *To Lord Ambrose, at Malfine.*

There was a thin thread of alarm in my mind, which would not ease. Something was on the loose at that farmhouse—something that stalked in the daylight.

I made ready for departure. I would probably not return for a few days, for I had business to do. At least some of the information that the gypsy-woman had given me should be taken as a serious matter. In my experience of these Romanies, with whom I have had something to do in my wanderings, they will keep faith if they trust you, and I did not doubt that the woman believed that what she had told me was important, and, furthermore, I must accept its truth. I am quite sure that Sir Anderton Revers would have thrown the woman aside, and if she had told him anything, he would have dismissed it as the babble of a witch. Sir Anderton had learned nothing in his long life.

There were some arrangements to make at Crawshay's. When I arrived at the farmhouse, Marie Crawshay seemed to be recovering from her shock, and from the effects of the dose of laudanum also, it seemed, for her eyes and manner seemed closer to normality and she was willing to listen to practicalities.

The immediate needs of a working farm had to be attended to, whatever was to happen in the long term. I suggested that a trustworthy manager could be found for the meantime, while the harvest was finished, the beasts looked to, the legalities settled. To install a suitable factor would take a few days of enquiries and discussions.

Marie assented to all these suggestions. Indeed, she was making further plans.

"No doubt Miss. Anstruther has been considering her future," she said. "I have no need of a governess. I will take sole charge of my son. This is his inheritance, is it not, Lord Ambrose?"

And she waved her hand around in a gesture that took in the house and the land.

Elisabeth Anstruther, I was told, was upstairs in her room. I wanted to speak to her, indeed, to tell the truth I longed to speak to her, but Marie informed me that she was resting and it would have seemed too unusual for me to press the point and demand to talk to her.

As I took my leave, I saw that the huge bloodstained table, where old Crawshay and Edmund had met their deaths, had gone.

"I had the men take it out," said Marie. She had followed me, and seen the direction of my gaze.

"My compliments, madam, that was a sensible decision. Mistress Crawshay, I will wait upon you tomorrow; may I suggest that in the meantime you get what rest you can. I shall be at Malfine; you may send word to me there if you need anything, and I will ensure that Tom Granby is well instructed to look after you here."

I bowed, and Marie mopped her eyes with a dabble of lace and nodded obediently.

"I thank your worship most kindly . . ."

Her voice trailed away. She gave a little bob of a curtsey and I swung up into the saddle.

I had some preparations to make at Malfine before I could leave it in the sole charge of Belos. I did not wish to subject Zaraband to the miseries of a Channel crossing and provision must be made for her care and exercise. Fortunately, I had acquired an excellent groom, who slept over the stables, though I normally made it my business to care for Zaraband myself. Nevertheless, for a short time, he must be entrusted with her. And then there were arrangements to be made for the transfer of the gypsy, who still reposed in my dungeons, to the castle at Anchester, where he would be tried at the assizes. He would thus be well away from this part of the world, where the whole countryside was roused up against him on behalf of the dead Crawshays, in a fit of morality which consorted ill with their unconcealed dislike of old Crawshay during his lifetime.

A message must be sent to the authorities at Anchester: I penned a few lines and Belos got them sent off; in reply there duly arrived a brace of stout militia men, and the prisoner was escorted by them, in safe custody. I could well imagine they were cursing me at Anchester castle, for allowing disturbances to erupt for the sake of a mere gypsy whose life was worthless anyway. Yet I had the power of my land and my inheritance, and if I chose to apply the law and insist they bring the prisoner safely to trial, they must needs make a show of willingness.

But the villagers seemed to have passed the worst of their passion for lynching the gypsy on the spot. He was led from the gloom of the Malfine dungeon to the cart, where, his hands tied behind his back, he was jolted along the august sweep of my driveway. When the cart passed through the wrought-iron gates at the entrance, a little gaggle of villagers was waiting and the usual unimaginative country curses were yelled in his direction; he stood silent, almost bewildered, as some gobbet of filth was flung at him. Like his woman and the child, he did not flinch as the driver whipped up the horse and flew through the little crowd. I heard that later, as the cart rattled through the streets of Callerton on its way to Anchester, a hostile mob gathered there also, for news of the deaths at Crawshay's had spread throughout the county now, but the driver had lashed out with his whip at a man who tried to grab the reins, and the cart swept on towards Anchester Castle, there to deposit its prisoner safely.

Granby must also be briefed, for the business which I intended would keep me away for some days, and the thought of the two women, Marie and the governess, alone in the farmhouse, was troubling. There, I thought, was a man I could trust.

"Belos, I need to send for Tom Granby, the fellow over at Crawshay's."

"Yes, my lord, I'll send the groom to fetch him. Another thing—my lord, you were enquiring about a fellow with a limp—there is such a man about, but no one knows who he is. I saw him in the inn yesterday, when I called in. A very thin man, dusty but with the clothes of a gentleman—and the voice of a gentleman too, as he called for some ale to be brought to him. Yet an odd fellow, a dandy turned poacher, I would say, for he was turning a poacher's snare over in his hands as he waited for his drink to be brought, and thrust it in his pocket as he took the mug. Perhaps he has been living off the land, catching himself small game."

"Did anyone know who he was, Belos?"

"No, my lord, although he was asking some questions. It seems he asked who was living at Crawshay's farm—but no one would answer him. You know how they are towards strangers round here, and one of the fellows told him roughly to drink up and be on his way."

"We need to be wary, Belos. Be on your guard here at Malfine—and I'll warn Tom."

I myself put a shotgun in Tom's hands when he arrived, telling him he would be well rewarded if he would continue in his post of guardian at the farm, and his honest, ruddy face nodded seriously in acceptance of his trust. He was a big man, Tom, and of a contained temperament, I judged, unlikely to be drawn into any village troublemaking by the hotheads such as Seliman Day who had led the attack on the gypsy. "And mind you lock up at nightfall, Tom. Let no one in after darkness falls. There is a stranger round the village, so they say, a man with a limp. Look out for him."

I did have some idea of the identity of the stranger who had been seen around the village, but not enough evidence to act upon my suspicions. The whispered secret, which the gypsy's woman had murmured to me as I rode away from the encampment at Callerton, was something which had intrigued me, like the governess herself. Elisabeth Anstruther believed that old Crawshay had been playing games of deceit and hatred at the farmhouse this summer, but if the gypsy-woman had told the truth, he was not the only one spinning a web of veiled and partial truths, of lies and counterplots. For the first time since my return from Greece, my mind was exercised, the murders at Crawshay's farm were stirring my curiosity—as the governess had stirred me sexually, beyond doubt.

For one thing, I was prepared to travel, to leave Malfine, which I had not done for months. The beast of life had lain up and licked its wounds, and was beginning to stir abroad out of its lair again.

INTERLUDE IN FRANCE

RIDING through the Normandy landscape, past orchards bright with enamel-red apples that had ripened early, on that hot summer's morning in 1830, I might have thought myself unobserved, but I know full well that the countryside is always full of eyes and gossip, though townsfolk may think themselves unnoticed. Boys scaring birds in the fields, an old woman taking her fowls to market—in reality, I am sure my every move was relayed, from the livery stables in Rouen, where I had hired the great white horse, Tonnerre, the best in the stables, to the moment I passed through the Porte des Cordeliers, the medieval gateway that still was the principal point of entry to the small town of Falaise. The town's chief claim to fame, as the ostler in Rouen had not hesitated to inform me, was the castle in which William the Conqueror of England had been born, and the bristling fortifications with which he and his descendants had embellished it.

That was the usual point of interest for visitors to Falaise, but I did not wish to inspect the local antiquities and had to disappoint the inhabitants with my lack of interest in their history: I enquired my way to the best inn in the town. Before I finished my soup at the Lion d'Or, my purse, clothes and breeding had all no doubt been assessed by shrewd eyes. I apprehended that the scars on my face seemed to cause some alarm at first, lest they indicate a villain intending some harm in the town. But when a couple of pieces of gold coinage changed hands in the Lion d'Or, I was correctly placed, with many smiles from the landlady, as a rich man, a visiting Englishman ("*Mais*, monsieur speaks French uncommonly well for a barbarian!") and a personage sufficiently discriminating about his food and drink to earn both respect and a generous hand with the post-prandial Calvados.

Like a civilised creature, I rested after my meal, and before dusk fell, strolled out into the Place Guillaume le Conquerant to take a turn about town.

There was no one in the church but an old woman, waiting outside a confessional to rehearse her heinous sins, and so, I deduced, able to observe me between her lace-gloved fingers as I strolled into the nave of LaTrinité. It was amusing to see how at first she, too, averted her eyes from my face, torn by white scars, but soon curiosity got the better of her, and she peered between her interlaced fingers without flinching.

I evidently behaved decently enough, at any rate for an infidel, and made sure to seem intent on admiring the balustrades of the gallery high above my head. When Monsieur le Curé appeared, I greeted him perfectly politely, although a nervous expression came over the priest's plump face at the sight of me—almost a blancmange-like cast to the good father's soft cheeks.

We began to converse, and I saw the old lady hastily cross herself and bow her head, pretending not to listen to our conversation, so that she could have seen nothing but my riding boots of chestnut leather, which she studied most intently.

As a result of my discussion with the curé, I paid a brief visit to the Hôtel Dieu, where the Mairie represented officialdom. There was a sour-faced clerk, whose name I discovered was Argenton. Argenton was an unamiable personage, hoarding his words like a miser, but I had a way of opening this tight-shut oyster. The clerk was probably an honest little sod, on the whole, but a gold écu seemed to slip of its own volition from my hand into his pocket, and he then shuffled off, to return with one of the great leather-bound volumes of the registers that remorselessly recorded the civil activities of the local inhabitants.

And not only the locals. There it was, the record which I sought, the essential piece of evidence that I needed to take the next step towards tracking down a murderer. I scribbled down a hurried note of the entry in the book, written in a sharp, slashing official hand, with the name of a notary beside it.

Immediately after my visit to the Mairie, I returned to the Lion d'Or and called for Tonnerre to be brought from the stable. The horse had a mouth as hard as a washerwoman's hand, and the space between his tufted white ears appeared to be stuffed as full of straw as his belly, but I had to make allowances: I was so accustomed to my delicate and brilliant Zaraband that no other mount could please me.

And so I departed back to Rouen and thence for Dieppe and the Channel crossing, leaving the curious eyes not much the wiser, though I am sure the fame of my riding boots passed into the oral history of Falaise. A great pale moon was in the sky as I rode away towards the coast.

CHAPTER 15

A farm boy arrived at Malfine, and his bare feet made tracks through the grass as he traipsed round to the back of the house. Watching from my bedroom window, I could see something that looked to be a letter clutched in his hand: no doubt he had been told to deliver it at Malfine, but had also been told he must approach by the servants' entrance at the back and should not dare to climb the steps of the great pillared portico at the front. I waited, idly, knowing the letter would be passed to me in a few minutes.

Sure enough, Belos duly appeared with a document, presenting it with a flourish on a silver tray; it still bore a grubby thumbprint which was doubtless the handiwork of the farm boy.

"My lord, a malodorous urchin has delivered a missive. I suppose we may be grateful for some signs of rural literacy."

I let this pass without comment.

I had somehow expected another communication from the governess.

But this was a different hand, an artless hand, not greatly accustomed to the habit of writing.

Marie Crawshay's letter, if not exactly elegant, was to the point.

"Your man, Tomas, has Disapered," she wrote. "I did not think you had Given him Leave to do so."

No, indeed, I had not.

"We have not seen him full three Dayes," her letter continued. "Word comes from the village that he has not been seen by Any Soule there. Would your Ld.ship be pleased to tell us if you have withdrawn your Protection from us."

I had been back at Malfine for less than twelve hours, and this was the first news I had had from Crawshay's farm. Belos, when questioned, knew nothing of Tom's disappearance.

I felt deeply uneasy: had I so seriously misjudged a man as to trust a fellow who would quit his post without a word and leave two defenceless woman unprotected? Or was there a more sinister explanation for Tom's disappearance?

There was something else which troubled me deeply, and that was the knowledge I had gained about the secret life of one of the inhabitants of the farm—something on which I would keep silent for the time being, lest the guilty should be forewarned of their unmasking.

Cursing, for I had counted on a rest before I resumed my researches into the little local puzzle that had intrigued my mind and distracted me from melancholy thoughts, I called for the mare to be brought round from the stables and swung up into the saddle, stroking the muscular silken neck of Zaraband. She was dancing and lively, keen for a run, though the groom would have exercised her in my absence.

As I was about to turn the mare's head away from Malfine, Belos appeared on the steps and hurried down towards me.

"My lord, are you going to Crawshay's?"

"Yes, Belos, in response to this communication from Mistress Edmund Crawshay." I waved Marie's artless note in Belos's direction. He took it from my outstretched hand and studied it. A curious expression came over his normally impassive countenance.

"My lord, there may be something amiss there. Will you not take a companion? At least take a groom."

I stared at the usually phlegmatic Belos. What had got into him? "What makes you think there is something wrong, Belos? Is it something you know, or just your unerring instinct for finding out the wickedness of human nature? I am hardly going into the mouth of hell, merely to a neighbouring farmhouse."

"Sir, I would say it was but the pricking of my thumbs. 'By the pricking of my thumbs, Something wicked this way comes.'"

"*Macbeth,* again, I believe. Belos, you're too damned well educated. I can't have a manservant who quotes Shakespeare—think how it would shame my guests—if ever I had any, of course."

"You are pleased to be witty, sir. But I do have fears, it is true. Last night the groom was woken by strange sounds—and he roused himself and looked out. There was a man on the edge of the lawn, he swears—a man who made off, hobbled off, rather, for he was limping. Who would come here like a thief in the night?"

"Why, a thief in the night, of course. That is the obvious explanation, and, seeing the household was vigilant, the thief in the night made off. It was some stray robber, and you, with the aid of a short-arsed groom, gallantly foiled his desperate attempt to carry off my family silver."

"Yes, my lord, but . . . Miss Anstruther—is she not rather a strange person? Might she not be connected in some way with the events that have occurred hereabouts?"

I was silent for a minute. I did not want to take Belos into my confidence as yet—at least, not until I had confronted Elisabeth Anstruther with what I had discovered in France, and given her a chance to explain herself. Was I prejudiced against her because of her unusual eyes, those yellow eyes which, as she had learned in her childhood, sometimes caused mistrust? I am a rational man; I set my prejudices aside. Or so I like to believe.

"She must indeed have been in a very nervous state of mind when she left here, Belos, but it was entirely natural—after all, it was just after the bodies of the Crawshay men had been found. An excess of sensibility, some young ladies would call such a nervous condition, and quite understandable in the circumstances, was it not? After all, she had been through a most frightful experience. A woman who has just seen two murdered men lying in the dining room is hardly likely to be of the most cheerful disposition."

"Yes, my lord. But still, I think somehow that she fears some discovery. I beg you to take care."

In Greece, Belos had saved my life. He had acted instinctively then.

"Well, I give you my word on one thing, Belos. I'll come to no harm—I assure you, I am in no danger. But this business of Tom's disappearance—that does bother me, I confess. I doubt whether they've made a proper search there. I'll call in at the village on my way to Crawshay's and get them to organise a search party—at least, in so far as those clodhoppers can organise anything. And some of the Crawshay farm hands can come on the search as well. I'll send you word if I need anyone from here. But I tell you one thing—they'll find Tom, even if they have to crawl over every blade of grass on their hands and knees."

I turned Zaraband away and rode towards the farm, preoccupied on the way with what I had learnt in my absence from Malfine. Elisabeth Anstruther, I knew now, had lied to me—or had not told me the full truth. She had concealed much in that document which had purported to be a frank account of what had happened since she had come to Crawshay's. Oh, she had told the truth about the atmosphere at the farmhouse, I did not doubt that. And she had told the truth about the quantity of blood around the murder victims. But she had not told me the truth about herself.

But was it for a sinister purpose, or for some simple human

reason, something that had no bearing on the murders, that she had kept things hidden from me?

I was intrigued by her, I confess it. I had not met a woman who puzzled me, not for many a long year.

It was almost dusk. The two women were in the parlour, the yellow light of an oil lamp casting sharp shadows over the low-ceilinged room. There was a deep tension between them—that much was obvious. The governess was turned away with her face to the window and Marie was staring at her as I entered the room, with such concentration that I think she scarcely noticed my entrance for a few moments. Then she swung towards me.

"My lord, it is so good of you to come! We are helpless here, the two of us, and Tom is still not to be found!"

She seemed much more composed than when I had seen her on the previous occasion, yet there was still a shrill note of tension underneath her speech. I saw the other woman turn towards me also, but the room was so gloomy that I could not make out her expression. She could not have guessed what my errand had been that had taken me away from Malfine for the last few days, nor in what way it had concerned her, yet I fancied there was something apprehensive in the way she greeted me with a few commonplace polite words. In this room, the most ordinary phrases seemed to take on underlying meanings, nods of the head seemed to indicate intensities only guessed at by an outsider. The governess's slight curtsey in my direction seemed almost a challenge to politeness, rather than an accession to social convention, so stiffly did she hold her back upright as she bobbed down.

The child was sleeping on the couch, wrapped up in a blanket. As I entered, he awoke, and uttered a little cry, and the governess crossed the room in response and would have bent down to tend him, but Marie thrust her out of the way with a strength that I had not supposed her to possess.

"Don't touch him!"

Elisabeth Anstruther started back as though she had been stung by some venomous creature.

I was surprised as to the hostility displayed by Marie towards Elisabeth, yet I had theories to account for it, not the least of which was that many entangled emotions lurked beneath the surface of the atmosphere in that dark farmhouse parlour.

The governess gave me a long look, I would have said a pleading look, with a kind of nakedness in it, and the moment beside the stream when she had put her hand on my shoulder came into my mind. I felt her long fingers again, as if they touched my flesh now, as if they burned, this very moment. Involuntarily, I looked down at her hand, and it was as if the movement broke a spell.

She turned, swept a curtsey with her silk skirt rustling in the silence, and left the room.

The child crossed to the window seat and began to play with a carved wooden horse. He seemed to have sunk into a world of his own and had barely noticed Elisabeth Anstruther's movement out of the door of the room.

"You look hollow about the eyes, madam. Are you not sleeping well of nights?"

"I cannot sleep much," Marie said, shortly.

"Would you not like a companion? Perhaps Miss Anstruther should share your room? That should provide companionship, a little society if you are wakeful at nights."

"Oh, no," she said quickly. "I keep my own room—with my son."

You lock your door and keep the governess out, thought I. Does instinct tell you to do that, Marie? Is it a natural inclination to protect your child? Or do you have some particular reason to be fearful?

Perhaps it was Marie's imagination that kept her awake. A woman who has suffered as she had done must have some terrible fantasies, dreams that would horrify the strongest of minds.

I thought of the stinking corpses I had seen in the out-house that stood a mere twenty yards away. Only a few flimsy walls between Marie and the bloody husks of her men. Until I had them taken away and laid elsewhere. What terrors might you have imagined, Marie, lying in your bed in this house?

Or do you share my knowledge? My new-found knowl-edge?

CHAPTER 16

MARIE wore a fresh cotton gown, as she had done when I first saw her, clean and uncrumpled. As usual, a faint scent of lilac came from her.

"I called in at the village to make some arrangements, Mistress Crawshay."

"No one has heard anything of Tom Granby for two days now. I have had the farm hands out looking for him, and sent word to his mother, but he has not returned home to her."

"I have given orders for a search. Some men from the village will come and we will cover the ground everywhere. I am sure you will have done everything that was in your power, but there may be places that have been overlooked."

"You fear something—something bad—has happened to him."

I was touched by her awkward, almost homely, way of putting it. But was she as simple as she seemed, for all the lilac perfume and the country ways, the "something bad" said innocently like a child?

"You will have no objection to a thorough search, Mistress Crawshay? Of the house, as well as the grounds and the farmland?"

"No, indeed, sir, of course I have no objection. But is it really necessary, do you think? I have already made them look in every possible place . . . and why should the house be searched? He cannot be here . . . Of course, no harm—let us hope no harm—may have come to him at all. So why do we need to hunt for him as if he were a wounded bird? After all, he is a grown man, quite well able to take care of himself."

"I assure you, Tom would not run away like a thief in the night."

"Oh, no, my lord, I did not mean to imply any such thing."

But you did, Marie, I thought. You did.

That's exactly what you were hinting at. That Tom had run off like a thief in the night. That he deserted his post. That he was wenching, or drinking country cider, or . . . I recalled the creature that the groom claimed to have seen from the upper window of Malfine during the previous night. No, that could not have been Tom; he had described a figure that was hobbling, limping, crippled in some way. I had my own theories as to that.

For the first time, a hint of dislike of Marie Crawshay entered my mind. Hitherto, I had merely been concerned for her safety. Now the feeling was more complex.

I continued aloud with the details of the search, as I had outlined them to the men in the village on my way to Crawshay's.

"I have told off two men to each field, and they are to search the hedgerows and coverts. And the ditches. And the woods. Those will take some time, of course, but the job will be done thoroughly. In the meantime, you will allow me to look around the house?"

"But I have already had it searched from top to bottom, from attics to cellars, and there is no trace of the man here, I assure you."

Perhaps she was subtler than I thought. She did not say anything that would directly discredit Tom. Perhaps a poisonous hint might come later: "Of course, there was a girl down in the village . . . I am afraid I have to tell you, my lord, that there is some silver missing along with Tom Granby . . ."

Why did I distrust her, the innocent widow, and not the governess with the strange eyes, of whom I now knew something that should make me watch her like a hawk, watch for every turn in her face, every expression that flitted across those yellow-grey eyes?

Perhaps I had misjudged Marie, perhaps she was not one, after all, to blacken a man's character when there was every chance that he might be as cold as the Crawshays in their coffins.

As we were talking, we had moved towards the window, and I could see her face clearly—a sweet and delicate face, open, one would say.

Looking out of the window now, Marie gave a start.

"I see there are men in the fields now, Lord Ambrose. Are they your searchers?"

I followed her gaze and saw two heads in the distance, bending onwards as they moved through a field of stooks and stubble.

"Are all your crops harvested, Mistress Crawshay? It will make matters much quicker if that is the case."

"No, only the long field stretching away down here. It is the most sheltered of all our land. The crops here always ripen first."

"Allow me to look about the house. I know you have searched already, but there may be some small thing overlooked that would perhaps tell us what has happened here. In the unharvested fields, the search will be long and tedious."

"You may look where you will, my lord. I have nothing that needs to be hidden."

I stepped out into the passage beyond the parlour door.

I had not previously explored the upper regions. Moving silently through the farmhouse, I thought I heard in the distance once or twice a child's voice, and then it called or sang some scrap of tune, and was silent again. Otherwise the silence was heavy and complete, broken only by the sound of my footsteps on the oak treads of the stair, the dry old timber creaking from time to time as I ascended. The heat seemed stifling, trapped within the house, at the top of the stairs, where I paused on the landing. Like most old houses, this was a rabbit warren, gradually partitioned and added to over the centuries, each generation forgetting the purposes of the previous one, so that store rooms, passages, bedrooms wound in and out, and little flights of rickety stairs led up here and down there. The farmhouse was not large, was indeed a poky place, of no consequence compared with a mansion such as Malfine, but it was so old that it was an elaborate maze of little rooms and closets. Door after door I opened, and then looked in at dusty emptiness, at trackless clouds of fluff and little heaps of soft rot or sawdust across the bare timbers of a deserted floor, and pulled close shut again with a soft click.

I stumbled up one little flight of steps to find myself in an apple loft under the eaves, the sweet, musty smell filling the air. In a few rooms, sheets were spread over the old furniture; in one such I picked up dried sprays of lavender that crumbled into powder in my hand.

In these rooms thick motes of dust danced in the rays of sunlight. Old, innocent, undisturbed. Like my mother's rooms at Malfine, shut up and silent. In fact, as the owner of Malfine, it might be said I was an expert, a connoisseur, of the empty room. I knew when there had been a recent presence, and when there had not.

Of the rooms that were still in use, old Crawshay's was obvious enough: the master bedroom, full of great pieces of black furniture that must have been there for generations, that might have been placed there when the house was built, in the era of that splendid and black-toothed Queen

Elizabeth. With a "z," unlike Miss Anstruther's "Elisabeth."

I looked around old Crawshay's place of repose—such repose as the ageing goat had enjoyed, and it was probably sound enough, for there had never been any sign that the old devil regretted any of his indulgences.

The black oak furniture was carved with Biblical scenes: an awkward half-naked Adam and Eve with bulky rustic fig leaves, a ship. There were figures in baggy hose and hooped skirts, trees with squat apples, serpents, fat dolphins that might do duty as whales. A huge carved oak bedstead. The curtains that had once hung round it had been taken down. Perhaps they were stored away in summer, perhaps they had simply fallen to bits and been dispensed with altogether. There was a big armchair in worn figured velvet brocade, the arms frayed and greasy, and on it lay a cushion of that old-fashioned embroidery our English maidservants had called stump-work, the little figures of some garden scene standing out, padded to raise them from the background, like some tiny creatures in a toy theatre. Their gilt trimmings had lost all their brightness and the greens and reds of the garden had all faded to the same shade of dusty brown.

It was a large room, yet the effect was cramped. I could not stand upright in it. Crawshay must have had to stoop also. He had been a tall man, probably of my own height.

There were candlesticks, a washstand, but nothing that spoke of the dead man. Nothing that might have been chosen by him, especially for use with his own living hands. There was a plain round shaving mirror, a long leather strop, brushes and accoutrements, including a cut-throat razor folded away and clean in its shagreen case, as I found when I took it out and examined it.

The dust seemed to thicken in my throat. With relief, I entered a little room next to old Crawshay's. A plain little room, with bare boards, a hard truckle bed and a night table. This was where Tom had slept. He had not been given the master's bed to sleep in, but an old servant's room nearby, within call should he be needed. Not that there had been any master to call when Tom slept on his hard and narrow bed, for the owner of this domain had been silenced and the throat in which that voice had sounded was now rotting flesh.

On the table were a candle stub and a tinder box. I could see no candlestick, but there were drips of wax on the bedhead: perhaps Tom had stuck the candle to the bedpost, as was the dangerous old country habit. Everything here was plain, anonymous, speaking of nothing, open in the whitewashed room, holding no secrets. Behind the door was a shirt on a hook. Plain, undyed linen. The stitching fine for a countryman's garment, with tiny white threads and rucks. Tom's mother had sewn it with a skill fit for gentlemen's linen, in spite of the coarse cloth which was all she could afford.

Tom might come back at any moment. His presence was strong, even in this bare cupboard that had served him for but a few days. He might walk into this room, tear off his shirt, throw his linen down on this horsehair mattress. Wash his big body here, stripped, sweating in the heat. Then reach for the clean shirt behind the door, pull it over his head. It was possible. Just possible. He might come back.

But I thought he would not.

I left the little room abruptly.

The other two occupied rooms were very much as I might have expected, except that in Marie's chamber there was no trace of her husband's garments or male accoutrements, such as shaving tackle. It had all been cleared away already. Marie was evidently not a woman to make shrines to the dead.

In this room, there was a little cot next to the great feather bed in which Marie slept. A painted wooden horse lay under the cot. Perhaps a trifle babyish? I tried to recall my own childhood. What toys had I, and when?

I opened closet doors, upon sprigged summer dresses, pretty but not elaborate. There were empty spaces, where perhaps Edmund's garments had lately hung. Had she packed her husband's clothes away? There was a charming little closet of rosewood, lined with green silk. Empty—no, not quite. At the bottom lay a small box with a clasp, though the owner had not troubled to lock it. Inside was a small bottle filled with a dark fluid and with a rough parchment label tied round the neck. Laudanum.

It was concealed from immediate discovery, but not really hidden. There was no reason for it to be locked away; after all, the drug was perfectly legal, although the newspapers daily chronicled those who had put an end to their sufferings with it, and those who had become slaves to its addiction.

A trunk at the end of the bed, and here were Edmund Crawshay's personal possessions, his shirts, breeches, a heavy cloak. Put away, the action of a careful housewife; put away, so soon after his death.

At the end of the passage was another room. I tapped on the door, and heard Elisabeth Anstruther's voice, low and clear, bidding me enter. This was strikingly different from the other bedrooms in the farmhouse: I could feel it as soon as I opened the door. The governess had succeeded in imposing her personality on it in a remarkably short space of time. New curtains of floral prints hung at the windows and a spread of heavy lace covered the bed. There was a deep window seat and the window looked out over a panorama of fields to a distant clump of trees. It was a place to sit and breathe in the atmosphere of the English countryside, and that was exactly what the governess appeared to be doing, for she was gazing out over the landscape, turning her head towards me as I entered. I begged her forgiveness for disturbing her.

"Search where you please, my lord."

She waved her hand around the room.

Again, I felt a current of sexuality, emanating from the traces of her body, her physicality, in this, her private room, as well as from her slanting yellow-grey eyes and her thin figure clad in sleek velvet. Disturbed, I looked around the room.

On the dressing table were plain silver-backed brushes and

tortoiseshell combs in silver mounts. They bore no mono-
grams, and were not new, but were made with an expensive
simplicity, displaying that fine elegance of which the best sil-
versmiths had been capable. And there was a fine calfskin
dressing case: no doubt that would contain the usual array of
crystal bottles for smelling salts and perfume and little silver
implements for the nails.

She crossed the room towards me and opened the case.
All lay innocently before me, each object nestling against
the lining of blue velvet.

"I have no secrets, Lord Ambrose."

"On the contrary, madam, I believe you have many. But
not in this room."

We stared at each other for a few moments. She read
something in my eyes—was it something that I knew, or
something I merely suspected? her gaze seemed to ask.

She turned swiftly to one side, and flung open the door of
a closet. "Pray search all you wish, my lord."

She ran her hand along the row of dresses, in a gesture of
tantalising intimacy, as if she were showing me her private
self. The clothes swung gently as she brushed them with her
hand, and irresistibly the vision I had imagined beside the
stream came to my mind, of her full white breasts naked under the velvet of her riding habit. I breathed in a scent, not
light and floral like Marie's. Something deeper and heavier,
with a muskiness, an animal note.

The clothes were all plain, in dark colours, suited to the
role of governess: plum, dove grey. High-necked, of fine-
woven wools and close-clipped velvet. Heavy, sombre: her
body would be hot beneath them in summer, and for some
reason this did not disgust me, as it normally would have
done, but the thought of her scents and her moisture attracted me like a flash of fire across the room.

"I know I am only a governess, but I am surely entitled
to some privacy," she said abruptly, although she herself had
willingly shown me the dressing case and the closet.

"I have no wish to distress you, madam."

"But you are too bold, sir, with my few possessions. You wish to go through my things as if I were some common thief?"

Even knowing what I then knew about her, what I had learnt in the interval since we last met, I admired her. She had a boldness I had not encountered in my dealings with women in England before. Of course, I had not been alone in a room with a woman for a long time—since before I got my wounds, and that was in another country. But from what I remembered of Englishwomen, they were either genteel or skittish, either coy or coarse. This woman had an independence as well as the certainty of sexuality promised by her long limbs, her bold eyes.

"Please leave me alone."

She said it suddenly, as if she had read my thoughts. She went on:

"I cannot leave Crawshay's soon enough, I assure you."

"That, at any rate, is doubtless the truth. You might be discovered for what you are."

"What do you mean by that remark?"

Suddenly there was a voice from the doorway.

"Yes, Lord Ambrose, what do you mean? Is Miss Anstruther not what she appears to be? I should not be in the slightest surprised, I assure you."

Marie Crawshay had appeared at the door, her face pale and her hands twisting together as she stared with animosity at the governess.

"Do tell us what you mean, my lord," she continued, and there was a ferocity in her voice. "I should long to hear it— in fact, I believe that as mistress of this house, I am entitled to hear it. Who are you, woman? What creature has been near my child?"

For the first time, I saw Marie in a quite different light; as a tigress faced with a threat to her cub. Her eyes were glittering as Elisabeth Anstruther faced her across the room. Through the window, I had a glimpse of the outside world: dark golden corn and clear blue sky, a world mercifully

empty of the passions and conflicts which filled this little
space beneath old Crawshay's roof.

But as the governess opened her mouth to speak, there
came a shout from downstairs—a rough countryman's voice,
calling urgently for me.

"My lord Ambrose? Please you to come, my lord?"

It was Seliman Day, the gypsy's principal tormentor. He
jerked his head in the direction of the fields and started off,
wiping his ginger scrap of moustache with the back of his
hand.

CHAPTER 17

WAYLAND'S Mound had never been ploughed. It was always left untouched, a long grassy knoll, with a few bushes growing scrubbily on the top of it. They were thorn bushes that formed an interlaced thicket at the very top of the mound.

There were many stories about this place in the district, some of which I recollected from my childhood, hearing them from maids whispering round the fire in the evenings, or from an old groom in the stables, too old to be of much use, but kept on for his knowledge of country cures for every ill that affects horse-flesh. I remembered his face now, as brown and wrinkled as a withered horse-chestnut. There were not many occupations on a winter's evening in the depths of the countryside, and scaring one another with stories about Wayland's Mound had been a way the locals could pass the time. There were dead men inside the mound, buried there after a battle. There was a giant buried in there, and sometimes he sat up and poked his head up out of the top of the mound, in the middle of the thorn bushes, and his great black eyes stared at you. He sang about his battles and if you heard him, you dropped dead. If you saw him, you dropped dead. There was a man from the village—why, my groom's grandfather knew him—who had been led there and offered gold by a fairy woman. He had plunged into the thicket after the cup of gold which she held out to him, and the thorns had torn his eyes out. Then he dropped dead.

The local people never went there after dusk. Hardly ever during the day, come to that.

Old Crawshay had jeered at these tales, I believe, and had sworn to have the mound levelled one day and be done with it, but somehow the project was never carried out. The labour and expense would have been enormous, and would not have been repaid by the small amount of extra land which would have been reclaimed for the plough, and so, year after year, the great plough-horses passed around it, and, year after year, the harvesters parted around its lower slopes as it stood up like an island in a sea of grain.

I myself had thought there might be some sort of burial inside, a burial not of giants, but of some poor old man-sized bones, something that had once been a human being, now harmless and unfrightening, to me at least, in death. The dead do not walk, do not sing. They have no powers over us.

Except in our dreams. There, they do have power, I'll grant you that.

Flies buzzed over the thicket in a dark cloud. Already, the face was beginning to swell and stain with the blotches of decay. The flies had alerted the searchers in the first place, the dark droning mass over the dry thorns. Soft slapping noises filled the air as we continually flapped our hands at the insects that rose, circled, settled again on our hands and faces. Someone had got a branch and was sweeping the flies from Tom's face, but they were settling again almost as soon as they were disturbed.

Tom wore a shirt and britches, torn and dirty. I knelt down by the blond head and gently touched it; it lolled to one side and a dark stream of liquid gushed from the nostrils and out over one cheek.

I heard a disturbance amongst the men who stood around me where I knelt beside the dead man, and saw that Seliman Day had broken out of the group and was standing with his back towards us, heaving, and the sounds of retching came through the fly-filled air. For all their brave talk, these were men who had never seen this kind of ugly death, this evidence of decay. I had, many times. I had seen it first when I was sixteen years of age, and then I had sickened and stumbled. Never since.

I knew the trick of it; to concentrate on this as if it were a piece of meat, to think of this human being as a complete stranger, as a thing, a mere lump of unfeeling substance, something I had never known in its warm and faithful life. I had not thought I should again feel this anger and sadness at the sight of death, and it was a new sensation, something creeping up in me like the sap in a drought-stricken vine. Tom, who had served me, was dead, and I was grieved, and that was the truth of the matter.

There was a puzzle here that must be solved. I tried to forget the sensations that washed over me and concentrated on facts, on the rough cream fabric of the shirt, and on the wounds beneath it. I saw three stab wounds, of about an inch across, and placed with a devilish accuracy, below the ribs on the left, so that the knife had struck upwards to the heart. Thick trails of blood had flowed from therein and stained the shirt. There were numerous small rents, ragged ones, some with thorns caught in them. The little cuts and tears made by thorns in the flesh beneath the shirt had not bled; dead men do not bleed. That is when the torturers give up, when they are no longer drawing blood. You cannot deceive them, cannot get a respite by fainting. As long as you are still bleeding, you are alive. When the blood stops flowing, they know they will get no more out of the victim, neither blood nor words, nor anything in this world ever again.

Tom had been dragged through the thicket after death; so much was clear from the scratches on his body.

I pulled the shirt together over the chest, and some objects flew out of a fold. Groping about curiously in the dry grass where they had fallen, I picked them up, small, heavy metal things. I felt round about with my fingertips and retrieved about half a dozen of them. For a moment I thought they were lead shot, but then I realised the shape was wrong. These were flat, disc-shaped, blackened, and some were misshapen. Some had fragments of scorched cloth adhering to them.

I put them in my waistcoat pocket, laid my kerchief carefully over Tom's face, got to my knees and brushed off the twigs and debris that had clung to my breeches.

"We'll carry him decently down. Go and fetch some planks or a trestle from the farm and then take him to the village. Wait—when you get to the farm, fetch the clean shirt from behind the door of his room and put it on him. And stop when you get to the stream and wash his face. Before his mother sees it."

They went off, crashing through the bushes and down the dusty little hillside, and I continued to contemplate possibilities, and impossibilities, for these were just as significant in trying to identify the murderer. Or murderers.

It would have been impossible for a woman alone to have brought the body here, up the steep slope of Wayland's Mound and through the thorns. Could two women have done it? It was just possible. Certainly a woman could have inflicted those wounds—of that there was no doubt. A sharp knife, at the right angle—in such a case, there was often little strength required. In fact, the victim often provided the force needed by lunging towards his attacker and impaling himself on the instrument of his death. I knew this, for I had been trained in this kind of combat, in silent, secret killing that needed cunning and cruelty, that demanded a cool mind and calculation, not crude physical strength. Take your enemy by surprise, attack him in cold blood, let him rush on to you, use his own strength against him—all these things I knew about, and by these means a great hulking strong man such as Tom Granby could have been felled by a woman. It was possible. I had known a woman in Greece who killed men, taking them by stealth.

The sound of men's rough voices broke through my thoughts, and the farm hands appeared, carrying a makeshift stretcher made from canvas lashed on to poles. They bore Tom carefully down the hill, trying to keep the dead face from being scratched by overhanging branches. They were surprisingly gentle with him, struggling with awkward balance to prevent the body from rolling off the canvas. I stayed for a few minutes more, looking at the lie of the land.

It would not have taken any great strength to kill Tom, supposing cunning had been used, but to get his body here? One person, one woman, could perhaps have got the body over the saddle of a horse, and led the horse under cover of darkness to the mound, and then up as far as the thorn thicket. To have dragged him through the bushes and hide him out of sight deep in the thickets would have needed a lot of strength—more than one person, almost certainly.

I thought of a quiet mare I had seen in the stable at Crawshay's, a sturdy country animal, so unlike that nervous equine aristocrat, my Zaraband, and imagined her shifting restlessly in the moonlight as a burden was dragged over her back, and a familiar hand calmed her and led her over the cobbled yard and out towards the open fields.

It was intelligently thought out. The murderer might well be right in thinking that it would be a long time before the body was found: after all, Wayland's Mound had a bad reputation locally, and the villagers stayed away from it. Safe from inquisitive children, safe from courting couples in search of a little privacy. An excellent hiding place, revealed only by careful and deliberate search—that, and the buzzing cloud of flies that droned above the thickets where the body lay hidden. Beelzebub, Lord of the Flies, claiming nourishment for his children.

Two women, working together, could have done it, if they could get the pony out of its stable and bring it to the mound. From then on, it would have been a bit of a struggle, but there would have been no haste if it had been done at night. They would in the end have managed to get up the slope with their burden.

I walked round the mound and saw on one side where branches had been broken off and a rough trail had been beaten towards the top. Easy enough, if one was prepared to hack a way through to the centre and then drag the body after. Easy if there were two?

Tom had been killed by knife wounds. Did that mean that he had not been murdered by the same hand that had killed the Crawshays—the hand that had fired the pistols in the farmhouse? Was the killer of Tom not the killer also of the Crawshays, old Gideon and his son Edmund?

Was a knife a woman's weapon, and the pistols that had killed the Crawshays more likely to have been used by a man? Or was it simply a matter of convenience? The same hand responsible for all three deaths, but finding the pistols ready to hand on one occasion and the knife on the next?

Some sharp knife, well honed by a careful housewife on the whetstone in a farmhouse kitchen, perhaps for cutting through sides of meat, for slicing the huge hams cured in smoke? A thin knife, that would slide into the flesh, long enough to reach the heart.

Suddenly, I knew what the scraps of metal were—the little discs that had fallen from Tom's pocket. I knew, and it was as if the tumblers of a lock clicked into place all at once.

They were the metal buttons from a woman's dress, buttons that would be covered with the same material as the garment. Those were the silvery splashes I had seen in the stove at the farm: the melted remains of such buttons, and they came from the same dress as the shreds of material in the ashes, blackened but still with a recognisable pattern, the fragments of a woman's dress.

A woman had killed Tom. I was sure of it.

I was conscious of something that was a strange sensation—something I had forgotten the feeling of, had buried somewhere many years ago, before the killings and the betrayals and the cries for liberty. It was anger, a slow-burning anger; I was angry for Tom, wanted to revenge him. Feelings that had been crushed out for many years were slowly reviving, like seeds in a desert that can lie in the sand for twenty years or more, and then put out shoots in the event of a freak rainstorm that soaks through the dried husks. This murder of an obscure farm hand, in a remote corner of England, stirred me into life; not just the death of this simple man, but the calculating cruelty with which it had been carried out.

I recalled the delay between the pistol shots of which the gypsy had spoken, that pause as he crossed a field on the way to the farmhouse. A pause of some five or ten minutes.

Did that imply that there had been two murderers, acting in separate sequence?

Or had the two women—Marie and the governess—had they operated together? Was their apparent mutual dislike merely an act to deceive outsiders—a show put on by two clever actresses? Or was their mutual hatred real enough, and their co-operation in a murder perhaps the uneasy truce of two enforced allies?

If Tom had been their victim, had that been true of old man Crawshay and his son?

Marie might have had a reason for killing the old man, but not her husband, who she would have hoped to inherit the farm.

The governess might have had some reason for killing Edmund, but the old man was surely her benefactor. She was employed on his insistence, after all.

The double death still made no sense, and Tom's demise did not supply any information that would solve the conundrum.

It did make it unlikely that the gypsy was the killer of the Crawshays. The three murders must be connected in some way—and the gypsy was safely locked up in gaol at some forty miles' distance. Had Marie lied in her version of events? But she had not claimed actually to have witnessed the murder, merely to have found the gypsy with the bodies of the murdered men. It might be that her interpretation of what she had seen was motivated by prejudice against the gypsy.

From where I stood, I could see the men trudging away towards the village with their burden. A veil of dust hung in the air, raised by the passage of Tom's rough and ready cortège.

I mounted Zaraband. We caught up with the men, as the sad little procession came to the village. I kept the mare in check behind them, watching as the men moved into the single street, with its huddle of houses. Then I walked her along, and dismounted. One of their number knocked at the door of a house which was somewhat larger and in better repair than most. There was no answer straight away in response to the knock, and he held the door open for his fellow pall-bearers, who entered with their inert burden, slowly, carefully manoeuvring it across the threshold.

The door was left ajar and I stood, opposite it. Through the doorway I could see bare whitewashed walls. There was an odd detail which stuck in my mind as trivial things somehow do at such times: a fiddle, hanging on the wall just inside the door.

There was a sudden, terrible scream from within the house. A woman's shriek. It seemed to echo along the dusty village street, a single cry, a sound as stark and fearful in that bare and empty road as in an ancient tragedy.

Seliman Day appeared in the doorway and leaned his forehead against the rough timber of the doorpost.

I crossed the street, and he looked around and saw me. We did not speak.

The screaming came again.

"His mother," said Day.

"Did he have a wife? A family?"

"No, only his mother. His father was killed at Waterloo. And Tom was her only bairn."

He moved away from the doorway of the house, and we walked along the street together, keeping pace for a little way.

"Reckon us'll miss him sore," said Day. "He played the

fiddle for us, did Tom, at weddings and that. Loved a bit of music, he did."

I thought of the fiddle hanging, silenced, on the wall of the cottage. Day paused, and struggled with his thoughts.

"My lord, I reckon whoever did for the Crawshays—that was the same as murdered Tom Granby."

"Aye, and the gypsy, remember, is locked safe away at Anchester."

Day looked up at me—he was a small man, standing a good few inches below my height. I saw with surprise that his rat-like eyes had tears in them.

"My lord, we did wrong there wi' the Romany, I confess it. He were an innocent man. But I ask you, find them as killed Tom, find 'em!"

We had reached the alehouse. "I'll go and tell them in there," said Day. "Gave them a tune many an evening, did Tom Granby. Maybe they'll do something for his mother. Them as can will help a bit. We'm not savages in these parts, though I saw by your face that you do think us so, my lord."

As Day turned into the alehouse, he stopped for a few moments and rubbed his dirty kerchief over his face.

The terrible sound of a woman screaming for her dead son was still audible at the end of the village street. It was the same sound in an English village as I had heard in a Greek one, and no doubt it had been the same in ancient Athens.

How little I knew of their lives, these English villagers! Less than of the Greeks among whom I had lived and fought—these people here, under my very nose, might be some kind of homunculi living on the moon, for all I knew of them. Yes, I was familiar enough with the outward details of their world—their crops, the way they built their wretched houses out of mud, for instance—but of their inner lives, their feelings, of the dead man who had played the fiddle, and the other who now wept for him on the threshold of the village pothouse, of these, I knew nothing.

At Malfine, I slumped into a chair. There was little time to spare—I must get back to the farmhouse before dark, for something was on the loose there, something that now threatened the two women who waited with the child for the night to come.

In a few words, I told Belos of this latest and, to me, most callous murder.

"His mother will be in desperate straits, my lord. She will not be able to pay her rent on her own—she had no one but Tom."

"Oh, damn it, Belos, see to it, will you? Get her somewhere to live on the Malfine estate—if that's what she wants."

"He was popular with the fellows in the village. Quite the village musician, Tom Granby. Played at all their feasts."

I had not been aware that Belos knew of this. Something occurred to me, something that I had not thought about previously.

"Belos, you know far more of them than do I. Do you not miss company, shut away here at Malfine, with a hermit such as myself? Is it not a sacrifice, on your part?"

"One that I am glad to make, my lord. I am too old to tread the boards of the stage again! But, to speak seriously, when you found me sick and starving in Greece, you saved my life. I will not leave your service."

There was a pause.

Belos added, almost as an afterthought, "I'll offer help to Mistress Granby, my lord, but the Granbys are a proud family—she may not take it."

"Offer it again, when winter comes and the winds are howling round her door. She'll take it then."

CHAPTER 18

I could see Marie's face looking out from an upstairs window of the farmhouse, gazing out on the countryside, as another woman had once done, many years ago, in that hot and barren country where I got my wounds. That woman, too, had dark curls tumbling round her neck: she too had tilted her head to one side with the very gesture I could now observe in the woman looking out of the farmhouse casement.

That woman in Greece had been a traitor. So traitors watched from their windows, enjoying the pleasure of seeing their victims as they walked unknowingly before them, beneath the walls of their houses, walking to betrayal.

I jerked my mind into the present again and chided myself for fantasising, for sinking into a reverie of the past. Marie Crawshay was the simple wife of an English farmer. Hate, treachery—all the elements that had entered into the Greek rebellion against the tyranny of the Turks—these belonged to another time, another place.

I walked up to the door of the house and rapped upon it. It was opened by Elisabeth Anstruther.

"Lord Ambrose . . . please enter . . . I'm afraid Mistress

Crawshay is resting . . . what is it? What has happened?"

I strode into the parlour and she followed me.

"Tom Granby is dead."

I could have sworn her cry of horror was genuine, that she knew nothing of poor Tom's killing, nor of how his body had come to be forced through the thorn thickets at the top of Wayland's Mound.

"Where . . . where did you find him?"

If she was an actress, she was a damned fine one.

"At the top of the Mound, yonder."

I indicated the long, dark shape of the hill, visible through the parlour window. And then I turned to look at Elisabeth Anstruther, and I felt again, although I knew I might be in the presence of a most cunning murderess, that powerful sexual urge that she had awakened in me during our encounter near the icehouse.

I did not care then if she had killed. I thought nothing of the corpse of poor Tom Granby lying lacerated by thorns. I wanted only to seize her, to press my mouth upon hers, to grasp at the firm white body that must lie beneath the chaste grey silk gown.

"My lord, did you receive the letter which I wrote to you?"

The words saved me, as I was in the very act of moving towards her, for they reminded me of the reason I must not trust this woman—the reason that had recently taken me away to France on a quest for the truth.

"I received it, madam, and I know it to be a dishonest paper—a document not worth the writing, for it conceals as much truth as it reveals."

"But I . . ."

"I have lately journeyed to France."

"I beg you, my lord . . ."

"Don't trifle with me, madam, I know all about your history. I have made it my business to find out about you. No one but ourselves need know what we speak about here, but I want some truthful answers from you."

In reality, one of the truthful answers I desired from her at that very moment, for what reason I know not, was whether she would come to bed, for again I felt that stab of desire, as she turned those strange yellow-grey eyes towards me. There was a despairing look in her face, a kind of exhaustion. She slumped into a chair.

"Ask what you will."

"Firstly, there has been something that puzzled me in the descriptions of old Crawshay in recent months. He was, apparently, something of a reformed character. He wore clean linen, left off much of his drinking, was less foul-mouthed than was considered normal by those who were accustomed to—how shall we put it?—the music of his voice. He was dressed in a fine tailored jacket when he was shot, when before that he wore filthy old worsted that had better served for sacking. So why should the old man change so? Was it, perhaps, connected with your presence?"

Her voice was very low, but steady.

"He wished to marry me."

"Marriage?"

"Yes, does it seem so extraordinary? He had been pressing me for three months before his death—urging me, trying to force me into it—almost threatening me—telling me I should be turned off without a penny like a servant-girl who has been dismissed if I refused him."

Those strange eyes were looking straight up at me now.

"Oh, I know what you are thinking, Lord Ambrose. He could have taken me by force—he could have had me as his mistress, perhaps. Why offer marriage to a penniless governess?"

"I think you would have refused to be his mistress. As to marriage—I would hazard a guess. The reason was Marie. He wanted to torment Marie. And the thought that there might be another child—a rival to little Edmund—a legitimate child whom Crawshay could make his heir whenever he pleased—that would have tormented her night and day, I imagine."

"Yes, I could see that, even when he asked me the first time. He made a point of telling me that the farm was not entailed—that he could leave it wherever he would. He could disinherit his grown-up son at the stroke of a pen. And I would be in charge of the household here. 'Marie need be of no more account than your servant,' he promised me. 'You would be the mistress here.' Of course, I could not accept him."

Her voice suddenly fell lower.

"I could not bear the thought of . . . of . . ."

"So did you refuse him?"

"I was afraid to absolutely refuse, in so many words—not just because he would have turned me out of doors penniless, for I beg you to believe, sir, that there are some things I value more than money—no, he was a violent man, quite unpredictable—I feared that. So I . . . I temporised . . . I begged him to let me answer him another time—and then another time . . . I gave him to understand that my family . . . there were hopes of a fortune in my family upon the death of a rich relation, but I must not jeopardise them by a hasty marriage . . . I held him off by every means I could think of."

She stood up now and faced me across the dark farmhouse parlour.

"But I did not kill him, Lord Ambrose. I was afraid of him, I even hated him. Yes, it would be true to say those things. But kill him, no!"

"Did Marie Crawshay know of his suit to you? Did she know her husband's inheritance was in jeopardy?"

"I did not tell her. It's possible old Crawshay might have done so—merely to torture her with the possibility. But if it was a motive for murder . . ."

"Yes, we are thinking the same thought. Marie had cause enough to kill the old man. But why should she kill her husband? He was putty in her hands, by all accounts."

The problem was gathering complexity. Elisabeth Anstruther had good reason for killing the old man—better than she had admitted, for I now knew the secret at which the gypsy's wife had hinted, and I knew the truths which

Elisabeth Anstruther had kept secret. And in those truths lay the seed of future fear—for her and for those around her.

Yet there was further cause to suspect Marie Crawshay. The shreds of burnt material with the still almost-decipherable pattern, the shreds I had found in the stove after the murders—they had been from a gown sprigged with a dainty floral pattern, exactly like Marie's charming country dresses. There had been no such garment in Elisabeth Anstruther's wardrobe—all her clothes had been of plain, expensive materials.

The shreds of cloth in the stove must have come from the same garment as the misshapen and partly melted buttons I had found upon Tom's body—which had provided the splashes of molten metal I had myself observed on the bars of the stove. So the same gown was implicated in all three deaths. And only one woman had gowns made from material with such a pattern, and that was Marie, though Elisabeth Anstruther was hiding a secret that I had discovered only through the agency of the gypsy-woman whom I had saved from rape. Yes, I could not discard the possibility that Elisabeth was involved in murder.

"You must realise that you and Marie, both of you, are in very grave danger—if anyone in the village so much as suspects that this household had anything to do with the death of Tom Granby, they will be roused against you. Tom was much liked in the village. There are many men there who were his friends, and they saw his body for themselves. I assure you, they will not forgive a murderess. I am afraid they may already suspect that you and Marie are involved somehow in his death—he died protecting you. Now, I advise you both to keep as quiet here as you can—stay out of sight and hope they do not think of you in the village. You will remain in your rooms tonight. Where is the child?"

"Upstairs, with Marie."

"Good. He must stay there. I shall stay downstairs."

As night fell, I was in the farmhouse, sitting in the parlour, in darkness. Inside it was sultry; my shirt was clinging with sweat. My pistol was jammed uncomfortably into the waist of my britches; I would have laid it aside on a table, but I was trained never to let a weapon lie beyond my grasp: I had seen men die because they had been taken by surprise. Outside shone the starlight of a clear summer night.

Upstairs, behind locked doors, were the mistress of the house and her son, and further along the corridor, the governess. The keys were turned in the clumsy old locks, on the outside, so they could not roam loose that night. The beasts were in their cages and the foolish zoo-keeper feared nothing. He had his pistol with him, however.

The heavy night was suddenly broken with a great flash of sulphurous light; those who were lying on sticky, sweaty beds, turning and tossing in the hot, wrinkled sheets, gasped and then sighed with relief at the approaching storm, as I myself had so often done.

I did not think there was now any fear of an attack upon the women by a village mob, for the weather was more effective protection than I could ever be: a man would be mad to venture out. It would cool almost any ardour to brave the night.

There was a pause, and then the whole night sky came alive again with a sheet of lightning. The landscape, so familiar by day, was as strange as that of the moon: black, white, grey, with scudding shapes, things driven in the wind, that suddenly came with a howl, sweeping over the countryside.

And the thunder started, great cracking echoes, that rattled round, repeated and faded, to start up again.

Inside the farmhouse, the storm drowned out almost all other sounds, but I could just hear Marie, pounding at the locked door of her room and screaming at the top of her voice:

"Lord Ambrose, I beg you, open the door. It's Edmund—he's only a child. He's terrified of storms."

I could barely hear the sound of my own footsteps as I ran up the staircase, of an old key scraping as it turned in a lock. Marie was standing there with the child in her arms.

The boy was indeed terrified. Every flash of lightning filled this room. The full force of the storm buffeted its windows.

We were preoccupied and deafened.

Then, only then, the rain started hammering down, like solid rods of metal. It would be drumming on the roofs, bursting through the ragged thatch of the village houses, gurgling in torrents off the leads at Malfine and forming a silver lake inside the great ballroom.

And there at Crawshay's farm the storm drowned out all other sounds.

CHAPTER 19

AS I turned to leave Marie's room, having unlocked the door so that she could bring the child down if she wished, all I saw was a flash of silver descending over my eyes—almost like a streak of lightning, another bolt of the storm that played about the farmhouse. Instinctively, I put up my hand, my right hand, in front of my face, and that was the action that saved me. I did not know what I was fighting, had no time to act logically. All I could do was to react instinctively.

My hand was being cut as if I had grasped hold of the thinnest and sharpest of blades, but one thing I knew: though my hand was being sliced to the bone, it was held up in front of my neck: it was protecting my throat.

I spun round, with the agony of my hand driving me on, and there came another flash of lightning and I realised what I was struggling against.

There was a wire noose around my neck.

Simple and cruel, but effective, a garrotte that would slice through my windpipe like a wire through soft cheese.

And pulling at the snare, choking the life out of me, was a thin, ragged creature, a man who stood unevenly before me, a fellow with a withered leg but with immense strength in his wiry arms.

The snare was something that he had no doubt learned to make in his wanderings, perhaps from the gypsies themselves, for as a horse-trader he had dealings with them. He would have used it at first when he was living rough in the countryside, for catching rabbits and other small creatures that fell into the noose and then struggled, cut and tore their limbs in the wire.

Then the thought must have come to him to use the wire as a snare for something larger.

But the game he had now caught was too big for him. This was no frightened, helpless animal. My hand was agony, it was on fire, slippery with blood, but still I held it up, keeping the wire from my windpipe, though I felt it biting round the side of my neck. I lurched straight across the room, driving into my tormentor, the torturer who had me on the cruellest of leashes, and my full weight fell against him, and he staggered backwards.

And there was another flash of lightning and I could see the man's visage: thin, hating, yet still a handsome face. "Oh Lucifer, son of the morning, how thou art fallen!"

I still relive those moments. My strength is waning as the blood pours from my hand and I do not manage to break his hold. Together we fall through the door of the room and roll down the staircase, and when we reach the bottom, the crippled angel is astride my back, wrenching back my head like that of an animal being made ready for sacrifice. The wire is biting into my throat now, throttling me, I can feel the blood roaring in my ears and my precarious hold on daylight vanishes as the world goes black.

Then there is another explosion.

This time, it is not thunder.

There is a smell of burning that is not the sulphurous smell of the storm.

I can see again. The pressure on my hand eases. A head with wet yellow hair, a blond and once-beautiful head, falls back. Blood gushes disgustingly from the man's mouth.

She stands at the top of the stairs, my pistol smoking in her hand. That pistol, fallen in the struggle, which she has picked up and fired.

There she is, with the weapon clutched tightly. She stands stock still, her skirts moving in the eddies and draughts generated by the winds of the storm.

The creature at the bottom of the stairs is not dead. He is dying, though. The pistol has shot him in the back: the blood pouring from his mouth has the frothiness of blood coming from the lungs. He turns his face and looks up the stairs.

The blood gurgles in his throat and his head falls back.

I go up the staircase and she is still at the top, staring, her eyes fixed, all the while, as I mount step by step, swaying with the loss of blood, and take the pistol from her hand. Without a word I enter her room, seize a towel, wrap it round my hand, and propel Marie gently through the door of her bedroom.

We stare at each other for a few moments: I am looking at the woman who saved my life.

"I know, Marie," I say. "I know who he was."

CHAPTER 20

❧ ❧

"HIS name was De Carme," I said, a little later.

That was afterwards; there was an anticlimax while Marie burst into sobs and I stammered my apologies.

"I'm so desperately sorry—how could I have mistrusted you so? I had got to the point of thinking you had killed your husband and the old man, fool that I am. I worked it out all quite wrongly, you see. He killed them both, of course he did. He came here looking for Elisabeth—burst in while they were sitting at the table, probably, and was half-crazed with rage and jealousy. And he must have killed Tom, too—perhaps Tom found him skulking round the farm and suspected him. The gypsy was incidental—he had the cursed bad luck to enter the farmhouse just after the killings, when you found him. He is a thief, perhaps, but not a murderer."

I had unlocked the door of Elisabeth's room—what a mistrustful idiot I had been, to lock those women in! I had carefully secured the victims under lock and key, while the real danger, the murderer, roamed unchecked.

So Elisabeth stood at the entrance to the room, as Marie sobbed with the intensity of her reaction, and I swung towards her and said: "His name was De Carme. Richard De Carme. He would have killed me if it were not for the courage of Mistress Crawshay here. Why did you not tell us of this—why did you not warn me?"

Elisabeth was silent for a few moments. Then she came in and put an arm around the shoulders of the weeping Marie, who pushed her away, as if rejecting a false comforter.

"I could not bring myself to tell you the full history of my unhappy love and marriage. Oh, I did wrong, I know that now, not to place the whole truth at your disposal, and write you a more honest account of affairs. But truly, I thought no harm thereby—merely that my feelings . . . that I need not disclose my feelings . . . But I will tell you both everything—you and Marie. First, let me take the child safely out of the room."

Marie had heard our conversation, and she stood up and herself picked up the child, who miraculously seemed unafraid and drowsy, and took him out of the room, to return a few minutes later.

"He's asleep! Oh, thank God he's safe! I care about nothing but my child!"

She sat down on the great feather bed and looked at Elisabeth with an accusing glance.

"You had better tell us everything. Who was that . . . that creature?"

It was a long story that Elisabeth had to tell.

"When I married Richard De Carme, he was not at all the man that you saw. He was full of life and energy then.

"His family had an estate in Normandy, and we met them often socially when my parents visited France. He was of a very good English family, but one with plenty of blue blood and little money. To tell you the truth, I believe they were living in France in order to avoid creditors in England. It was not long before my parents withdrew from their society, for they did not approve of the De Carmes' way of life. The young men, Richard and his brothers—they would bet on anything, not just horses. It seemed that anything that came along might be cause for a wager; they gambled on sports, on prize-fighters, on the number of puppies that might be born in a litter, on the bumpers of champagne that could be consumed at one sitting, on anything that could be punched, kicked, jumped, swallowed, thrown, fired or caught.

"Of course, there were quite a few English exiles of this sort in France. Every year you will read a few lines in the paper, recording that some such Englishman has shot himself or poured acid down his throat, or been killed in a duel, in some town such as Dieppe or Boulogne, after being reduced to indigence and no longer supported by his family. You will recollect that Beau Brummel, once a leader of fashion and companion to the Prince Regent, was reduced by his debts at the last to a filthy old creature living in a French boarding-house, his one remaining worldly delight being to creep along to the pâtisserie for custard tarts, when he could beg a few centimes from some English visitor.

"Not many exiles suffered such a spectacular fall as Brummel. And I, an innocent girl, did not at all understand that might be the fate that awaited young Richard De Carme, as handsome as an angel, so gallant. His exploits, his wagers and breakneck rides across country, the duels and the drinking—these all seemed to me, who was from the most cautious and prudent of homes, quite dazzlingly worldly: I thought Richard De Carme could give me all the sights and excitements my quiet upbringing had denied me. In short, I fell helplessly in love with him.

"My parents were extremely worried, I realise that now. Richard was mightily prepossessing; he had the most charming manners of any creature I have ever met, and my mother nearly succumbed to them and might have agreed to our marriage. But my father was adamant, suspecting Richard of being a mere fortune-hunter. I was forbidden to see him, forbidden to write, or to have any form of contact whatsoever with any member of the De Carme family.

"Well, you know what young people are like. When my parents forbade me to see Richard, I fell deeper in love with him than ever before. One morning during a visit to Normandy, when Mother wondered where I was and why my bed had not been slept in, she found that her daughter, with what little jewellery of my own I possessed, and a fast horse from the stables, had vanished into the night. Oh, I desperately regret it now, that I was so foolish, but I had continued to correspond secretly with Richard and it was not difficult, with little bribes here and there, to find servants who would carry messages between us. And bribes were not always needed, for there are always foolish old hearts around to indulge young people and carry on intrigues where they suspect affections are blossoming. The middle-aged are flattered by being taken into the confidence of the young, I fancy. My French godmother would not forbid us to meet at her house, and so we laid plans, until at last I left my parents' protection and joined Richard, as I thought, for all our years to come, for the rest of my life.

"We headed towards England, thinking to put the Channel between my parents and ourselves, and determined to marry at the first place we could stop."

"That place was a small town near Rouen," said I, "and I have seen the record of your civil marriage in the registers of the Mairie there. 'Elisabeth Madeleine Anstruther and Richard De Carme, both being persons of English nationality, on the fourteenth of September, eighteen twenty-eight.'"

She was astonished. "How came you by this information? I thought I had kept my marriage secret from all the world."

"You and your husband stayed in Falaise above a month, for a particular reason, I believe."

"Why, yes, we had but a few guineas between us, and Richard thought to make some money at horse-trading. He thought he was a famous judge of horse-flesh, and it was the pursuit of a gentleman, after all; Richard could never resist a horse-fair. His idea was to purchase and break in some foals, and then to breed up some fine hunters and carriage-horses, and take them over for sale in the English rings, where he might see a fine profit. He had been conversing with the ostlers in the auberge at Falaise, the Lion d'Or, and he had learned—"

"That there was a great horse-fair shortly to be held at Guibray, just outside the town . . ."

"You are a magician, my lord! How did you divine all this?"

"Never mind, I'll tell you later. Go on—what did your husband do?"

"He watched the parade of horses going through their paces at Guibray and picked out two fine black animals that would make a perfectly matched carriage pair.

"He did not discover for some days that he had been cheated, and that one of the horses had white socks which had been dyed black, to persuade Richard into thinking he was buying a perfect pair.

"So there was the biggest part of his profit gone, and worse, he had been made a fool of. I had never seen him in a rage before: he cursed and shouted and hurled his glass to the ground—he was like a child in his fit. Still, I thought it was but one occurrence and that he had some cause, for indeed he had been cruelly gulled.

"Well, he sold the horses for what he could get and we made our way to England, fearing pursuit by my parents if we remained in France.

"Then we began the restless life of horse-traders. From fair to fair we tramped, and each time trading down, each time losing a little more of our tiny capital, staying in inns of lower and lower quality.

"My husband was not equipped for such a life of poverty and restraint: he bore it ill. Several times he lost his profits by foolish purchases. Sometimes he drank too heavily, and then he was so fuddled a child could have deceived him.

"Our small funds dwindled and dwindled till at last I knew not where to turn to pay the reckoning in the humble taverns where we stayed in the poorest rooms. My small stock of jewellery was soon dispersed and my husband's way

of life promised no improvement in our fortunes; that was
something I understood within a few months of our marriage. Of course, I appealed to my family in desperation. But
they were deaf to my entreaties and not even my mother
replied to my letters.

"There were dark shadows now in my husband's mind; he
drank to keep them away, but they redoubled after every
drinking bout. He picked quarrels, harped on grievances.
He got an injury to his leg falling under the hooves of a terrified mare in the stables of an inn. He was too drunk to get
to his feet.

"Within a year of our marriage, I had nothing left for
him but pity, as he spent his nights raging and weeping and
his days in the taverns. I believe it might be a hereditary
weakness, for his grandfather, so I have heard, was thus. Finally, my husband took to blaming me for his ill fortune,
and said I had brought him bad luck, that he had won nothing, had no success at any wager, had made no profit, since
he had met with me.

"I will not say that he had no love for me, for perhaps he
did when we were first together, but when he understood
that my father would really do nothing for us, that my family would pursue their coldness towards me and that no help
would be forthcoming from that direction, then his talk became wild and full of hatred. He turned so against me that I
was sometimes frightened to move or speak when the fit of
anger was upon him, and I spent one whole night sitting
bolt upright against the casement, fearing for my life.

"The next day, I fled. I gathered together a little money
in my purse, which I had obtained by selling to the mistress
of the tavern some of my clothes, my lace and my kid
gloves, which I could never have occasion to wear. Below the
window, I could see a stagecoach preparing to leave the inn
in the early hours of the morning. I cared not what its desti-
nation might be, and took a place as far as the coach would
travel. Thus, the next day, I found myself in the marketplace

at Callerton, with scarcely enough money for a few days' lodging, and I knew that I must get some sort of work to keep body and soul together, but what employment might I expect? I could think of nothing but that I might offer my-self as a governess.

"Yet what respectable household would take me in, with my history? I imagined my own mother, confronted with the prospect of engaging someone with such a story as my own. 'Quite out of the question, I'm afraid. The girl has no charac-ter to show me, no references. She has never undertaken any employment of this kind before and has no experience of children. She has been disowned by her own family. And she has a drunken and disreputable husband whom she has aban-doned. What is she, wife or widow? How can we take such a person into our house?'

"That is how any mistress of a household would have spoken, I assure you. So at Callerton, where I put it about that I was seeking a position as governess, when old Mr. Crawshay engaged me without question, I could not re-fuse him. I would have to use the last coins in my purse to pay the landlady, and after that I must go with Crawshay or starve. I had sold my wedding ring already, so he saw no ring upon my finger, and he did not know my story—he took me as governess for his grandson without question, though I believe he had his own reasons for doing so. But he knew nothing of my marriage. I myself tried to forget what I had been through.

"But then I suspected Richard was trying to track me down. Perhaps he thought I might give him some money— I'm very sure he did not follow me through love. He could have made enquiries at the inn where I left him, and so eventually traced me here."

"Was it he who locked me in the icehouse?"

"Yes—I believe so. I think he had trailed me from the farm that evening when I came to the icehouse." And I, even though I knew she had deceived me, longed to stroke the long, loose strands that tumbled round her shoulders, I involuntarily reached out my injured hand towards her, forgetting the pain of it. I had recognised those fine threads of hair as soon as I had seen them on old Crawshay's body, so alert was I to her physical being, to every hair that sprung on her head, to every movement of her flesh, every drop of her sweat, even. But I held back, as she continued her story.

"Yes, I think he followed me, and to imprison you in the icehouse would have been exactly the kind of joke he enjoyed. He would have laughed, I think. He found dead things funny. And dying creatures, too. He laughed at them. He enjoyed looking at them. But he was not a killer—no, I did not believe he would kill."

She shuddered and pulled her chair closer to the fire.

"But why did you not tell me?" I asked her. "You hid it all from me and I found out the truth only because the gypsy's woman told me where to go for the evidence of your marriage. You see, the gypsies get about far more than we know. She and her husband had been travelling about trading in horses and donkeys, and had been at that same fair near Falaise. It's a famous attraction for the Romanies; they come to it from far and wide.

"They knew all about the trick played upon your Richard. He was well known among the horse-traders as a gull who fancied himself with bloodstock, and the gypsy-woman had seen both of you several times, at your lodgings in Falaise where you stayed during the fair.

"They have a strict sense of honour, the gypsy clans. I had saved her man's life when he might have been murdered by a mob at Crawshay's farm, and I had given her my protection to get her safely away to the encampment at Callerton. She believed she owed me a debt, and the only way she could repay it was with information. She told me of the governess at Crawshay's, that mysterious woman whom she had seen before, at the Normandy fair—oh, you and your husband were the topic of much talk there, I assure you, and it was known that you were but newly married, in the town of Falaise.

"On the night when I took her to safety, that gypsy-woman told me of the place to seek evidence of your past history: it was thus she repaid me the favour I had done her, as best she could. And she was warning me, too, for they knew your husband was a man of uncontrollable temper."

Elisabeth answered passionately, turning towards me and uttering the words with great feeling.

"Truly, I thought he was harmless—you must believe that. I thought he was mad, quite mad, sick in mind as in body. Would you let them put him in Bedlam? No, I see by your own face that you would not, that you think as I do on that subject—you have seen them in Bedlam, have you not? Chained in their own filth, while the paying visitors jeer and the gaolers poke them through the bars, prod them like animals so they will jump and squeal and show off their tricks, those wretched lunatics. No, I thought perhaps I could get him sent back to France, get him looked after by his family. I had loved him once, you see. He did not kill the Crawshays—so why should I suspect that he would kill any-one else? He raved and threatened, but he had never killed anyone in his life.

"In a way, it was I who caused the deaths of the Craw-shays, because I concealed my marriage to Richard, and so when old Crawshay proposed marriage to me, he thought his suit would succeed and that I could become his wife. Oh yes, I am sadly at fault, Lord Ambrose, for concealing my past when I came here, for trying to make a new life for my-self. I should have understood that you cannot make a break with the old life—that is merely self-deception, is it not?"

Yes, it is, thought I, and you are not the only one, Elisa-beth Anstruther, to have loved not wisely but too well, and to have tried to escape the weight of your past actions. It is self-deception indeed, and I also am guilty of it. I have tried to bury myself here in the English countryside as if I had never loved and fought, never suffered the smart of betrayal, as if I were a thing of clay whose passions are all long dead.

There was a sound from Marie, who seemed to be crouching down on the bed, whimpering.

"I'm so tired now," she was murmuring. "Please, my lord, let me get some rest. I don't understand at all how you could have thought that I had killed them—that I was a murderess! Why, I have never harmed another creature in my life—except just now, to save you!"

I hastened over to her. "And very courageous you were too, Mistress Crawshay, and I thank you with all my heart. I did think that the murderer must be a woman, I confess, for a particular reason: I found some buttons from a woman's gown in poor Tom Granby's shirt—and there were shreds of a dress such as you yourself wear in the stove downstairs, as if someone had tried to burn a stained garment. I leapt to a totally unwarranted conclusion: that a woman with a sprigged cotton gown had got the blood of the murdered men upon it, and had tried to burn it for fear of discovery."

Marie's face seemed very pale now, her voice faint. She had plainly suffered a frightful shock, and I knew that I should not keep her any longer from her rest, yet she spoke again, murmuring softly:

"Oh, Lord Ambrose, but I fear you were partly right! You see, I had taken my husband, my dear Edmund, in my arms when I found him lying there, and afterwards I realised that there was indeed blood on my gown, and I . . . well, I feared that people might think me . . ."

"Might think you guilty, as I was fool enough to do!" I cried.

"Yes, might think me guilty," she repeated. "And also I did not want my child to see the blood and perhaps be terrified at the sight . . . So I quickly pulled it off and put on a fresh one—it was the work of minutes. And then later, after everyone had gone, I just cut up the old gown and burned it. That is all there is to confess, sir, that is the end of the story."

"Forgive me, dear Mistress Crawshay," I said. "Now get some rest, I beg you. There is nothing more to fear."

Marie turned her face into the great pillow of her bed, and Elisabeth pulled the coverlet over her.

"I fancy she's taken some more laudanum," she said, as we slipped out of the room, leaving Marie to sleep. "But she must get some rest. And let me bind up your hand."

We built up a great fire in Elisabeth's room, for both of us suddenly felt chilled to the bone in spite of the heat of the summer's night. Elisabeth was suffering from shock, and I from loss of blood. She tore some linen into strips for bandages and bound my wounded hand. The pain eased away.

We sat beside the fire, until I grew impatient of talk.

My mouth was suddenly on hers and we began to caress each other slowly in the firelight, her gown slipping off and the lace-fronted petticoat beneath it, till we lay before the warm flickering flames, both utterly naked, our bodies moving, first she on top of me and then I lying over her, till at last we had shuddered and gasped together.

CHAPTER 21

A little later, we heard a disturbance from Marie's room, and I pulled on some clothing and went to her.

She was awake: the slumberful effects of the drug had not lasted long, and she was thirsty and restless, reaching for a flask of water that stood beside the bed, the noise of which, as it overturned under her uncertain hand, had alerted us.

Elisabeth brought a jug of water from her room and Marie drank thirstily. She sat up on her bed, propped on pillows, great dark circles under her eyes in spite of the rest she had enjoyed.

Feeling that she was in need of a restorative, I offered to fetch her some wine from the decanter downstairs, and she gratefully murmured her thanks.

There was something else I must do when I got to the bottom of the staircase, something which I did not mention to the women. The body of Richard De Carme lay at the foot of the stairs, where he had fallen. I went down the stairs, dragged the dead man into the parlour and pulled off the shawl that lay over the piano on the other side of the room.

It was getting lighter. That was why I saw it there, just as I was about to fling the shawl over the white face. A flash of red and yellow pinned to his jacket, the cheap, swaggering colours somehow pathetically bright. Someone, I supposed, some woman, probably, with a laugh and a joke as he passed through the fairground, for this was such a favour as they give away at fairs, to entice the men to part with their money, trying their luck at shooting stalls or at fisticuffs with some travelling pugilist . . .

I stopped dead.

Fragments of conversation whirled round in my head.

Elisabeth, saying of her dead husband: "Richard could never resist a horse-fair."

The gypsy-woman I had taken to safety at Callerton, telling me why the Lees had camped near there: "To sell their ponies at the Callerton fair."

And that had been on the day after the murders.

What day had the fair taken place?

I tore up the stairs, and without ceremony burst into Marie's room.

Marie lay with her eyes closed and Elisabeth was holding a wet cloth to her temples. The curtains were drawn, but the currents of the storm were whirling through the gaps in the old casement windows, and candles flickered wildly in the draught as I entered, their light glancing round the room, illuminating dark corners, gleaming on polished wood and the small silver and glass toilette adornments around the room. Marie was propped up on a mound of white pillows, and the pale faces of the women leapt out of the gloom in the fitful light.

Marie opened her eyes with a start and both women were astounded by my frantic entrance. I seized Elisabeth by the shoulders and said to her, passionately:

"When was the fair? The horse fair at Callerton? Which day was it?"

She gazed at me in amazement, but answered my question quite calmly, as if she were humouring a lunatic.

"Why, it was the day Edmund and old Crawshay were killed. I remember it so clearly, because the fair was all along the streets, so it was difficult to make one's way through the town. But I was not interested in it—I just carried out my purchase and came back here to the farm—I came back in the cart, as I told you. I forgot all about the fair—I did not think to mention it."

He must have seen her there. He had followed her from the fair. Followed after her, on foot, and arrived on the outskirts of the village, where I had seen him creeping along like a guilty creature, moving low down behind the hedgerows. I had believed that he must have tracked Elisabeth down by enquiring after her, but it all fell into place now. He had simply seen her by chance in Callerton, had probably followed her through the streets, and seen the direction the pony and cart had taken when she drove out of the town and turned into the road for home.

Aloud, I said:

"He could not have killed them. Richard De Carme could not have killed the Crawshays, because he was at the fair that day—and he has a fairing—a rosette—in his buttonhole. He could not have got here on foot the same day, and arrived before you did, because he could not have overtaken you on the road. But the Crawshays were dead by the time you got home—when Richard was still following you! So someone else killed them. Someone at the farm. I do not believe it was the gypsy. And I cannot, will not, believe that it was you!"

Marie sat looking up at us as we embraced before her eyes, and it must have dawned on her that I would not believe any attempt to throw the guilt upon my Elisabeth.

There was a long silence as she realised that the myth of her innocence had been utterly destroyed.

Then she started to cry out denials, to protest that she knew nothing at all of the matter, that she was innocent of any shadow of wrong-doing. "Please, I beg you, my lord, be so good as to fetch me the little bottle in the cabinet there.

I must . . . I feel so dreadfully unwell . . . I beg you, sir, I plead with you . . ."

I knew what she wanted. The latest dose of laudanum was ceasing its effect. I could see shivers running over her skin and a sweat dabbling her throat and forehead. Her hair seemed damp and clung to her head in thick tresses.

"Tell me everything that happened here on the day of the murders. Then you can have some of your . . . medicine."

It was cruel, but I had to go through with it. Let her get to that little blue phial of laudanum and she would be once again calm, tranquil, a smooth and accomplished liar. This was the only way to make her speak, the only way in which she could be forced to tell us the real story at last. I knew now what had happened, but it was all conjecture: we must have it from her own lips. A confession.

And the only way she could be made to confess was to keep that tantalising opiate, that blessed peace and oblivion that the drug would bring, away from her lips.

There was a long silence, broken by sobs from Marie as she realised I would not yield. She looked pleadingly at Elisabeth, who exchanged a glance with me, and then silently shook her head.

And then Marie started talking, twisting her hands, talking as if she could not stop, as if it were some strange life blood pouring out for the last time and she could hold nothing back. She was, by this time, quite mad. She told her tale as if she could see it, as if it were happening right there in front of her eyes, like a story in a play.

CHAPTER 22

OLD Crawshay is laughing, with his head thrown back, his mouth fully open, showing his strong teeth. He is laughing especially at Marie tonight.

He has just told Edmund and Marie that he is to marry their governess. He is enjoying himself, watching his family react.

Edmund is stunned at first, then begins to ask silly questions, such as when will the ceremony happen and what bedroom will the newly married pair occupy. Edmund doesn't count.

But Marie counts. Marie knows what it means straight away. She sees that the governess is strong and healthy, that old Crawshay has plenty of sap left in him. There will be children.

And then what will happen to big Edmund and little Edmund, her husband and her child, and at present the heirs apparent?

Why, they will be displaced by the heirs of the governess. By the children of the woman Crawshay brought home from a fair, and Marie's own child will be made to share his inheritance, might even lose it altogether. Crawshay will not favour little Edmund over the children the governess will bear him. Marie knows that in her bones.

What does she say now when the old man announces his news? Marie is a dangerous person. She congratulates him on his engagement.

That night, she pictures the future to Edmund as they lie sleepless in the feather bed. Their son will be dispossessed, themselves passed over. At best, they will be reduced to the status of second-class citizens in the kingdom they expected to inherit. They could even be turned out of doors by those shadowy ghosts of the future, the children of Crawshay by his second marriage.

At last, even Edmund understands what is happening. It penetrates slowly, but the danger finally sinks into his brain. And Marie works on that. Night after night, as the huge harvest moon rises over the fields and the heat of the day spirals away in draughts of hot air escaping up to the sky from the parched ground. When Edmund reaches for her in the feather bed, Marie turns from him.

Marie believes the governess will be mistress here soon. Between themselves, they still refer to her as the governess, though Crawshay has said that she is no longer to instruct little Edmund—after all, it would not be right for the future lady of the house to perform such a menial role.

Crawshay enjoys telling Marie that. Edmund sees his wife taut and full of bitterness.

Prompted by Marie, Edmund begins to think of his own mother. Did that gentle creature not suffer intolerably at his father's hands? How many times did Edmund tell Marie the story? How he, as a child, just like Edmund, came running indoors one day to find his mother, her beautiful hair pulled loose and spreading over the floor where she lay, her mouth dabbled with blood. And Crawshay standing over her.

Oh yes, the old man had destroyed Edmund's mother. And now he was to remarry as if she had never existed. As if she had never been, never suffered, never borne a son to inherit. Was that tolerable?

Night after night, in a whisper, Marie talks to her husband. Night after hot summer night. The heat now is extreme, the greasy meat washed in vinegar to sweeten it, the milk tainting quickly in the pan, flies gathering wherever the men in the field stop and gather to eat their rough bread. The flies drink their sweat.

Only the very early morning is cool. Every morning, Marie goes into the byre where Mattie is doing the milking. One cow is allowed to keep her milk: she is suckling little Edmund's pet, a gold-furred calf. The boy goes with his mother every morning, to watch the quiet beasts shuffling in their straw.

Crawshay in the old days would never have permitted such a thing as a favourite calf, petted and spoiled. He would have put a stop to it straight away.

But Crawshay is absorbed wholly by his governess. He forgets about his family, so that he scarcely bothers even to victimise them. He certainly does not keep an eye on what they are doing.

Edmund realises that it will really happen now. The marriage that may annihilate his chance of inheriting the farm and its land. His wife will be overruled, will have to obey the governess as mistress of the house, and his child will be displaced by the governess's children.

From time to time, old Crawshay stokes the fires.

"Won't be long now! She'll have me soon enough. Wish me joy, son!"

Edmund backs away from his father.

"Wish the bridegroom all happiness, Edmund, my lily-white boy!"

There is a pair of pistols in the outhouse. Once they were fine weapons, but now their duelling days are over and they have gone down in the world, like the Crawshays themselves.

The silver inlay on the butts is tarnished. They are too fancy for old Crawshay's taste. He would mock them as the mere adornments of a fop.

Marie brings them to Edmund. They need cleaning, she says.

Husband and wife look at each other, a long, silent exchange.

Edmund rams oily rags in the barrels. Marie polishes the silver butts. She breathes mist on them. Rub, breathe, rub, till silky, watery gleams of silver come to the surface of the metal.

Edmund finds ammunition. Bullets, powder.

It is the hottest day of the year so far. The governess has gone to Callerton in the pony-cart. The Crawshay family is alone at the farm.

The light is blinding outside the house, and inside the air is thick with motes of dust. When Crawshay comes in from the fields at noon, a cloud of insects follows him.

Crawshay does not wish to spend the hottest afternoon of the year out in the fields. He intends to do the farm accounts—after all, he will soon have to afford the expense of a wedding, as he tells his son and daughter-in-law with great relish.

Edmund is blinking as he follows his father to the hall. Crawshay goes ahead of him as he sits down at the dining table. As Edmund turns his head to the light in order to look at his father, he sees flashes of red as the sun beats on the thin skin and the veins of the eyelids.

Old Crawshay is laughing at some secret pleasure of his own as he sits at the head of his own table, in his own house.

Marie has followed the men into the room.

And puts a cool and lovely pistol into Edmund's hand.

The last expression on Crawshay's face is amazement. The princess in the fairy story, whose pet toad turned into a man under her very nose, could not have been more astonished than Crawshay, when he sees the pistol in the hand of Edmund, that feeble, soft, pretty boy.

In a way, you could say that Crawshay is spared all fear at the end, since he dies disbelieving.

His blood begins to dry almost as soon as it runs out, clotting dark and velvety over his breast: steam rises from it.

Marie moves before Edmund does. She comes towards him and he thrusts the pistol at her, holding it out desperately as if begging her to relieve him of this burden, as if he scarcely knows what he is doing.

She takes the pistol from his hand. A smell of burning, coming from the barrel with wisps of smoke, makes her wrinkle her nose. She lays the pistol on the table.

Then there comes a long pause, while Edmund clings to her, asks her, "What shall we do?," whines in terror at his own actions, shakes and shudders in her arms, till she pulls away.

She has put the pistol down.

And from the dresser beside her she takes up its twin.

She takes it up because of those hours, again and again, alone in the middle of the night, walking the house, contemplating the nature of the man she has married, finding relief only in the little phial of laudanum. She does not intend to kill Edmund, does not scheme for it nor long for it, does not spend hours day-dreaming of it, as she did of the old man's death.

She takes up the pistol because Edmund is babbling, terrified, because she knows he will not keep silent, that he is the weakest of creatures. She despises him, as utterly as his father did. She hates their life together now, wants only to be left alone with her child, and with the laudanum bottle when she cannot hold back from it, as happens more and more now.

But now the opportunity is here in front of her. She can be entirely free, unburdened by that stupid, demanding, babbling husband; she and her small son can live at Crawshay's with no one else to gainsay her wishes. Chance has put this in her hand and she will take it.

She takes up the second pistol, still unfired, and turns towards her husband.

Her arm jerks upwards as she fires, and Edmund jerks backwards, and then the puppet Edmund folds up over the table.

A little later, the gypsy calls at the farmhouse asking for a drink. Although he heard two shots from the direction of the farm, he sees nothing amiss. The house is neat, the doors all shut, the curtains drawn against the flies and heat.

"Did I hear gun-firing, mistress, as I walked through the field yonder?"

"Aye, my husband is out after coneys."

Marie has laid some old shirts, bundled up, on the kitchen table. The gypsy may have them—they are cast-offs.

And wrapped carefully inside the parcel of linen, deep inside, is a little bundle which she has made to put inside the bigger one. In this there are a couple of gold guineas. And though of course there is no way a gypsy could honestly have come by those same guineas, she wants to make doubly sure. So she has added Crawshay's silver watch, unmistakable, initialled: a dozen persons will swear this was old Crawshay's own timepiece that never left his weskit chain. She did not need to deliberately smear it with blood, for a stain got upon it as she was pulling it out of the old devil's pocket.

There is a smell in the air, but the smell of animal blood is not uncommon on a farm and the gypsy thinks nothing of it.

He thanks the gentle Mistress Crawshay, departs.

The governess will be due back from Callerton very shortly.

Marie's preparations are almost ready. There was blood on her gown, but she has changed into a fresh one. The stained dress is taken into the laundry room, the fire beneath the boiler lit, the dress fed into the flames. It must be cut up and put into the grate scrap by scrap, to make sure it is all consumed in the flames, but there is not much time left now and some of the pieces are thickly folded together and do not entirely burn.

And she has forgotten the tiny round pieces of lead covered with the material of the gown—the buttons, some of which melt into little silver splashes, which Lord Ambrose will note. And some of which are only partly melted, forming little misshapen discs.

Which Tom Granby will notice with puzzlement when he rakes out the ashes of the grate, thinking to spare the ladies of the household that dirty task. Tom picks them up, not knowing what they are, meaning to ask Mistress Crawshay if they had been thrown in the fire by mistake.

He puts them inside his shirt.

And Ambrose Malfine will take them from Tom's body, and will know that a woman killed him.

Soon, Marie will go and discover the bodies. She will do so as soon as she hears the sound of the pony and cart returning from Callerton.

CHAPTER 23

"AND then, you see," whispering as the candles guttered, murmuring her story with a terrible detachment, as if she was explaining some moderately unpleasant task such as the wringing of a chicken's neck, "and then, you see, I had to do it again. It was your man Tom that time. He began to be suspicious. I came down to see to my dress, the one I had cut up and put in the fire of the boiler. I had not had an opportunity to make sure it was all burnt, you see. There seemed always to be someone with me—Elisabeth, or you, Lord Ambrose, or Tom. Until that night—that was the first chance I had to slip downstairs. I don't know how I awakened Tom. He was sleeping well, I thought, I looked in his room and he seemed fast asleep. But it was a hot night. Perhaps he was restless.

"I went downstairs to make sure all the scraps of my dress had been burnt away in the stove.

"But Tom must have woken up and followed me. I heard someone coming down the stairs and slipped behind the door, and then Tom came into the laundry room. I saw him looking at the boiler and the stove, and then he got the poker and raked around in the ashes, and then he was holding something up in his hand, holding it up to the moonlight. I could see what he was holding quite plain. There were some buttons and a scrap of cloth in his hand.

"From my dress—the one I thought had all burnt away.

"Then he turned and went back up the stairs to his room.

"So I had to do it to him. Because he was on my track. I could see that. Tom might catch me and the gypsy-man might go free. Poor Tom, sad, wasn't it? But you do see why I had to do it.

"It wasn't so difficult. I couldn't use the guns again, not with that yellow-eyed woman in the house to tell all the world she had heard a shot in the middle of the night. But I used a knife. We've all seen pigs being killed, when the butcher comes round, haven't we? I knew how to do it."

Marie suddenly began to giggle.

"And something else as well—I thought I was very clever. Now you won't be shocked, my lord, will you? Do promise me you won't be shocked, sir. How do you think I solved this problem? I mean, the problem that had led me into this fix in the first place. The blood on my clothes. After all, it was in trying to get rid of a bloodstained dress that I had given myself away in the first place, was it not? So I knew I mustn't make the same mistake again. What do you think I did?"

She broke off into a fit of laughter.

"I took off all my clothes. Every stitch! There was I, running round the farmhouse stark naked in the night! It was wonderfully cool. I stood there, naked, for a while before I got on with what I had to do. Do you want to know where I got the idea? There was a story going round the village of Mrs. Philp of Brighton who was lately tried at Lewes Assizes. She got a maid from the workhouse and took her clothes away and made her serve the dinner and clear away the dishes and dust the parlour—all stark naked! Imagine it!

"Anyway, I realised that going naked would be the best way for me, for blood is easier to wash away from skin than from clothing, is it not? But, like a silly creature, I stood there, wondering about how to get Tom Granby back down from his room.

"Then of course I knew what to do. I just walked up, bold as brass, without a stitch on. I opened the door of his room, and stood beside his bed and touched his shoulder.

"Oh, you should have seen him, the great booby! The look on his face when he opened his eyes and saw me standing there! As if he had never seen a naked woman in his life—well, perhaps he had not, my lord, unlike you gentry, with your grand pictures of nudes all on show in gilt frames. I daresay all he knew were the dirty petticoats who uptailed for him behind some pothouse."

She stopped and laughed again.

"So I ran out of the room and downstairs. And, of course, he followed me, exactly as I knew he would! How could he know there was a woman with no single stitch of clothing running about the house in the dark without being tempted?

"He came looking for me. I was waiting at the bottom of the stairs. I picked up the knife first from the kitchen, then I went to the stairs holding the knife behind me, and when he came down I pressed myself against him all naked as I was. So of course he didn't notice the knife. And I jabbed it where I knew his heart would be—it went in quite easily and he fell on top of me. And then I wriggled out from under him and I was covered in his blood, of course."

She paused for a moment or two and slid her hands up and down her body.

"So then I went and washed it off under the pump in the kitchen. And poured the water away. I ran upstairs and put on a loose nightgown. And that was that. Or so I thought."

"How did you . . . how did you move him?"

"To Wayland's Mound? Ah, there I had the most wonderful stroke of luck. I could never have moved him on my own, you see. He was a great big man, Tom Granby, far too heavy for me. I thought I would have to make up some story about how I had found him lying there, in his own blood!

"But then it was all so fortunate. At least, that was what it seemed like. Everything I was praying for seemed to come true that night. Tom had followed me downstairs just as I wanted, then the knife had killed him just as I had planned it would. And my clever idea of taking my clothes off—that was just right, too.

"I thought it would be better to get the body out of the house—then there would be no suspicion of me, you see. It would be thought that someone outside the house had killed him. I tried to drag him along. But I couldn't move him at all, you know, he was just far too heavy. I tried, yes, I did. But I couldn't. I lifted up both his arms and tried to pull him along. But it didn't work. I was just going to give up when I heard someone moving about.

"Well, I was frightened then, I can tell you. But I had a sort of confidence, too. I had just killed one man, weak though I was. Why should I fear another?"

Why indeed should Marie fear? I wondered. It was De Carme, I supposed. De Carme come looking for his wife, who was going under her maiden name of Anstruther. She was living as Elisabeth Anstruther in this very farmhouse—anyone in the district would have told him the name of the governess at Crawshay's: there could be no turnip within a fifty-mile radius who had not heard the scandalous details.

So De Carme had come here at night, in search of his Elisabeth. For what? For revenge? Perhaps to ask for her help? We would never know.

Marie was talking again.

"It was that man called De Carme. The one who was here again, the one you were fighting. But that first time, he broke in then, too. I heard him, scrabbling at the door, and then he crept in."

To see her crouching over a body.

They had made a monstrous pact, the two of them, over Tom Granby's dead body.

"I could accuse him, you see. All I would have to do would be to say he had broken in and I had seen him standing over

Tom's body. It would have been just the same as I had done with the gypsy. They would have arrested him straight away. But on the other hand . . ."

"He could give you away. And they might have believed him," I supplied.

"Exactly. You see things so clearly, my lord. Who would believe the word of a gypsy against me? But this might have been different. I could tell that this man had been a gentleman once—he still had that in his voice, his manner—and he might have had powerful friends or kin. He was not like some wandering Romany whose life mattered not a scrap to anyone of position. This man was more dangerous. I had to come to some arrangement . . . We made an agreement. He would help me with the body.

"He was stronger than I thought, for all his crippled leg. I got the pony out of the stable—I kept her on the grass, so her hooves wouldn't make any noise. And then we got Tom on her back—we pulled him over her back, between us. I was very frightened then, I must admit—it seemed to take so long. I wanted to tip him in a ditch, somewhere nearer, but then I thought of Wayland's Mound. No one goes near places such as that, for they are believed to be cursed by the Old Folk, and the body would never be found there. And it did take a long time to find it, didn't it? I hadn't thought of the flies. The flies gave it away in the end.

"By the time we got the pony back in the stable, it was almost dawn. There was one more thing to do—I had cursed old Crawshay many a time for keeping those old flagstones on the floor, instead of having timbers laid like everyone else, but you may be sure that I blessed the stone floor then! It was quite easy to get the blood off."

"You said there was a bargain. What did he gain from it?"

"He was to come and go here secretly as he pleased. I was to give him food and shelter—and money if he needed it. I had to agree to whatever he said, didn't I? Or else he could have told people what he had seen. But I knew that once he had helped me with the body I was a lot safer. Because then he was an accomplice, wasn't he? He couldn't inform on me without involving himself. They would have said, 'Why didn't you tell us straight away, this tale of seeing Mistress Crawshay at night, pulling at the arms of a dead man.'"

Again there was that high-pitched giggle.

"But to tell you the truth, I was always afraid that he would give me away. The threat of it was always there. So when I shot him, as you were struggling on the stairs with him, I didn't really care which of you I hit. Because I knew that you, my lord, were getting close to the truth, so it would keep us both safe, the cripple and me, for a little longer if I killed you. But if I hit him, I would silence the witness against me. Either way, I thought I would gain. People might have thought I had shot him to save your life. But I didn't: I took a chance!"

Marie began to laugh, the laughter that you hear at puppet shows, the laughter of a cruel child who sees Mr. Punch hitting Judy over the head. It stopped abruptly, and the room was horribly silent, except for the rustling of the curtains as they lifted and sank in the draughts that blew about. Suddenly Marie sat up in the bed and clutched at my hands with her thin fingers.

"Get it for me, I plead with you, get it from the closet."

She sank down on her pillows, spittle staining the lace that trimmed them, but she was still whispering urgently, harshly. "I beg you, sir, bring me my little bottle of medicine from the box in my closet. Let me have it now . . . please give it to me . . . oh please, I beg you. I have told you everything now, there is nothing more."

I turned to Elisabeth. "We can allow her to have a little laudanum now." There was a small silver spoon in an old-fashioned gilded wine glass, on a table beside the bed.

"Give her a spoonful from the bottle in the little box."

Then I thought of the child, Edmund, brought up with the notoriety of being the son of a murderess, of the boy perhaps hearing from some tavern idiot of how his mother met her end, how she was turned off the ladder on the scaffold and kicked her legs in the air as she choked in the noose.

And of something that might be even worse—of the men who had menaced the gypsies, of how they would react in the village if they found out that Marie was the murderess. She had killed not only the Crawshays, but Tom Granby, Tom, the carpenter who had played the fiddle at the country feasts and weddings—he was dead, and by Marie's hand. I did not know if I would even be able to get her to Callerton if they came for her from the village. I had saved the gypsy— but with Tom's help, and he was no longer at my side. God alone knew what they would do to Marie if they learned of her guilt and laid hands upon her.

"You can't stay forever in a nightmare," Marie had said to me, "you must wake up some time." Waking or sleeping now, Marie was forever in that nightmare.

I took the bottle from Elisabeth's hand as she was about to pour out a spoonful of the laudanum. "Let me do that— do you fetch a cloak or something to put around Mistress Crawshay's shoulders when we take her downstairs—why, there is such a draught here!

"I have to make some arrangements," I added, as Elisabeth was leaving the room. I took care to speak with my mouth close to Marie's head, so that she must hear my every word. "I'll have to get Marie to Callerton—they take women prisoners there. She'll be among the drunken hags, the petty thieves, locked up in Callerton Gaol. They sleep on dirty straw and sell themselves to the turnkeys merely to get food. And after a few months of that hell, she'll be taken out and put up on a scaffold, and they'll put a hempen noose around her neck and hang her."

I saw by Marie's terrified eyes that she was visualising what kind of existence there must be in store for her, once she was taken out beyond the walls of this room.

The door closed behind Elisabeth.

"You know what I must do, Marie, for I am sure you can still understand me. There will be a little time before I take you from here. You may make your preparations."

I still remember her eyes as they looked up at me, her lids swollen and empurpled with weeping. The little silver spoonful of ruby-brown opiate was halfway to her lips. She understood.

I placed the bottle beside the bed and left her there.

CHAPTER 24

WHAT I had done was not right, I know; I had prated virtuously about law and justice to these country clod-pates.

But it was a human thing to do, and I had begun to rejoin humanity.

"I did not think she would take so much," said Elisabeth, later, "but I suppose she had an almost-full bottle of laudanum, the one I had brought from Callerton."

This was after we had found Marie, curled up in the great feather bed that her Edmund had bought to enjoy his wife in. The bottle of dark-blue glass lay on the floor, where it had fallen, empty, from her hand. Her eyes were closed; there was no trace of life.

Elisabeth and the child I took to Malfine, for they could not be left in that house.

"What of the gypsy?" she asked me. "He is still in the gaol at Anchester, is he not?"

"I shall write a report for the authorities," I said. "I will say only enough to secure his release; there is no need to expound upon our personal histories."

She understood that I was assuring her of my discretion, and nodded her head. Elisabeth had not told me all the truth, yet I myself could not pretend to any greater virtue, for had I not replied in kind? I recalled the words I had spoken to her, there by the stream as she traced my scars with her fingertips:

"I fought in Greece. For Greek independence."

So I had, but it was not the whole story. Like Elisabeth's account, it was a partial truth. I found myself admitting something I had never before confronted: I did not fight for the purest of motives, solely for the restoration of ancient liberties to a country in chains. I fought for human love, for a woman, for my mother's claim to land, for all the mixed bag of earthly motives. Who am I to condemn Elisabeth Anstruther because she withheld the truth from me, when I have deceived myself for so long?

I continued:

"But what of you, where do you desire to go now?"

"Oh, I have nowhere."

"Perhaps your father will take you in—if he knows what has happened, that De Carme is dead."

"I will not ask him to."

"That is what I had hoped you would say. You need somewhere to live. Young Edmund needs someone to look after him. Come to Malfine, both of you."

"You would have such an infamous woman under your roof?"

"With alacrity! It will be the talk of the turnips! And we might even open Malfine again—at least, those parts that have not entirely fallen down!"

What I fought for has long gone, in any case. Perhaps I have a life here in England after all, among these country timber-heads who are my own kind.

We shall see, Elisabeth Anstruther and I, we shall see.

About the Author

Jane Jakeman is an art historian who has travelled in the Mediterranean and the Middle East and has had numerous articles on art, food and travel published in newspapers and magazines, including the *Independent, The Sunday Times* and the *Guardian*.

She studied English at the University of Birmingham and has a doctorate from Oxford University in the architectural history of Islamic Cairo. She lives in Oxford and is at present on the staff of the Bodleian Library. She is also writing her second Lord Ambrose mystery.